Praise for Jenna Bayley-Burke's
Pride and Passion

"The writing is fantastic, the character development is brilliantly done, and the pace of the story is excellent...don't miss your chance to read Pride and Passion."

~ *Long & Short Reviews*

"Lily and Jake's rocky romance is a pleasure to read."

~ *The Romance Studio*

"Pride and Passion is a beautiful read with each character evolving and having to address their pride as the story progresses. Jenna Bayley-Burke brilliantly entertains the reader with this romantic love story. Enjoyed immensely."

~ *Single Titles*

Look for these titles by
Jenna Bayley-Burke

Now Available:

Her Cinderella Complex
Par for the Course
Compromising Positions
Private Scandal

Pride and Passion

Jenna Bayley-Burke

SAMHAIN
PUBLISHING

Samhain Publishing, Ltd.
577 Mulberry Street, Suite 1520
Macon, GA 31201
www.samhainpublishing.com

Editing by Heidi Moore
Cover by Scott Carpenter

First Samhain Publishing, Ltd. electronic publication: March 2010
First Samhain Publishing, Ltd. print publication: February 2011

Dedication

Let other pens dwell on guilt and misery. Jane Austen.

To the Busy Bee Moms—Helen, Jennifer, Kris, Naoko, Nora & Tonya. For helping me push through the baby brain and find myself again.

I ask nicely, but she refuses. What does she want me to do—beg? Beauty & The Beast

Chapter One

Drizzle hung in the air, hovering without falling. The gray sky held back its tears just as she did. Her father's lawyer held a black umbrella over them both, but it didn't keep the moisture in the air from seeping into her clothes, chilling her to the bone.

Lily Harris concentrated on breathing, not wanting to listen to the pretty words she doubted anyone meant. She was grateful for weather as bleak and melancholy as she felt. It fit. It might even keep the vultures in the press from getting a good shot.

That's what she'd been reduced to since her father's death, now that his tawdry secrets had spilled onto the tabloids. They wanted a picture of the poor little rich girl left alone with nothing but scandal. She didn't want to give them the satisfaction, and yet she didn't know how to keep it from happening. Even the people who cared enough to attend the private graveside service were probably waiting for the headline of tomorrow's paper, waiting to gossip about how she looked and acted today.

She took a deep breath and held her head higher. She might not be able to go without weeping at home, but here

Lily was determined to exude such pride none of them would dare even hold her gaze. She glanced about the crowd, watching the tactic work on everyone. Everyone but Jake Tolliver.

Instead of mixing with the throng, he stood to the side looking down on them all. His height gave him that advantage over people, as did his bank account. But neither could buy him the social grace necessary to know to look away. He held her stare, but not with tender sympathy. Jake's gaze was filled with nothing but mocking coldness.

His dark eyes stormed as he watched her, his chiseled face immobile. The man was beautiful to look at. Like a marble statue, he was gorgeous but chilling to the touch. If he thought she'd break now, he'd never get the satisfaction. Lily would not look away. She couldn't show the fear that seeped into her whenever she felt his heavy stare on her.

The young minister moved to console her, breaking the connection. His words rang empty, everything did. Each word seemed veiled with morbid curiosity of how a world so tightly woven could unravel so quickly and completely. There was nothing left of the life she knew. Everything would have to be sold to clear the debts, and even that might not be enough.

"If there is anything you need, Lily, even just to talk..." The kind expression on the minister's face almost jostled her stoicism. It might have if she'd met him before today.

"That is kind of you." A deep masculine timbre vibrated through her, but Lily refused to turn her head and look at Jake Tolliver. She might make a spectacle by asking what gave him the right to speak for her.

"Lily will be well taken care of. I'm sure you can understand her need for privacy." Jake's hand was firm on her elbow, turning her from beneath the relative safety of the umbrella. With him so close, vulnerability crested within her like a wave, not breaking until she couldn't return to her father's gravesite without making a scene. Shaking off his firm hand would have the same effect, and he knew it.

"It's time to go." Jake kept walking, which propelled her forward. The drizzle in the air prickled at her face, leached into her lungs.

"Not yet," she managed to whisper, casting her glance back to where workers had stepped in, covering the still-open grave with a tarp. It still seemed so undone, so unreal.

"He wouldn't want you to stay, Lily. Not to watch this, to be watched." His body and determination dominated her, kept her feet moving though everything in her wanted to remain.

"As if you would know." She laced her voice with venom but kept her face calm. "You have no idea how this feels. I doubt you've felt anything in your entire life."

"I have broad shoulders, Lily." His voice was colder than ice and his fingers tightened on her arm. "Go ahead and take it all out on me. But for your own sake, wait until we are in the car. These people are watching you, and the press is waiting at the gate."

She pursed her lips into a firm line, hating that he was right. Lily Harris was newsworthy now, especially if they got a picture of her mid-fit. A few weeks ago being in the paper meant she'd attended a charity event, and now it symbolized how low her father had sunk before his death. What a legacy to have been left.

Jake walked her over the marshy grass of the cemetery to where rows of black cars waited. A curt nod of hit head banished the car she'd arrived in and its driver. Before she could ask what he was about, he opened the door of the only car with color in the line, a shimmering emerald green, the signature color of Tolliver enterprises. His hand was firm at the small of her back, urging her inside. Just as the chauffer had acquiesced, so did she. No one dared defy Jake Tolliver, the cold and forceful. At least not under the watchful eye of the media.

Jake joined her in the car and turned the key, the feral sound of power echoing in her ears. The car leaped onto the road, racing out of the gate amid flashes of light.

Jake watched the rearview mirror carefully, speeding through the side streets along the route he'd planned. Every parasite knew where they were going, but he didn't care to be followed.

Lily sat ramrod straight, her blonde hair damp around her shoulders. Even now, with her world crumbling, she looked perfect. She was every inch a woman, and yet she still radiated a child-like innocence that had him doing things for her he'd never even consider for someone else. And she hated him for it.

He tightened his grip on the steering wheel. Lily would need to get over that. He had to protect her now. The alternative wasn't even an option.

She took off the sunglasses shielding her eyes and folded them carefully in her lap. His glasses. She hadn't thought to bring any, and he hadn't wanted to risk her crying in front of the vultures who'd come to the service to pick over the carnage of William Harris. To her credit, she hadn't shown any sign of weakness, none anyone who didn't know her as well as he did would notice.

"I don't know why we are bothering with trying to keep away from the reporters. They'll be at the house anyway."

"The house is gated for a reason."

Lily let out a long sigh. "We can't lock the gate. What will people think? It'll make a bigger fuss if we screen everyone before they come."

"No one is coming to the house. They've had enough of a show for today. Besides, you're not up for people who claim to be your friends prying for information."

"That's not the way it works, Jake."

"It is today. After we arrive the gate will be locked and guarded until all this dies down." He downshifted as he entered the exclusive neighborhood. Ten houses set far back on sprawling plots of land, all held for generations. Buying a house here was unheard of. He'd been the first in decades. "Anyone who is truly your friend will understand, and you don't need the rest of them." He swung into the drive, his scowl softening at the two burly men standing in front of the gate. What the iron bars couldn't hold back, he knew these two would be able to handle. Being in the construction industry came in handy when you needed a job done quickly and quietly.

"It's just not done, Jake. People will be offended."

"Good thing for you I'm not a slave to social niceties." With a nod to the men, he passed through the gates, relaxing a bit when he heard them close. She was safe here, for as long as he could get her to stay put. "Your politeness and civility can't protect you right now. Life isn't a party, Lily. You should have learned that by now."

"Of course, all I know how to do is waltz like a proper lady and design a seating chart." She stared out the window, her delicate jaw clenched so tightly he thought she might crack a tooth.

"You have led a spoiled and sheltered life," he agreed sardonically. "If you listen to me, you will make it through this. Your father was my friend and I'll do anything to make sure you're protected."

Lily sniffed. "Does that include from you?"

"Do you really fear me?" he mocked. She did, he'd known it from the first time she had to shake his hand. But he was through playing beast to her beauty.

"I don't need protecting, and I don't need you trying to run my life."

"I'm not trying, Angel. I'm doing it. It's for your own

good." He parked the car and killed the engine.

"You have no idea what's good for me."

"Of course I don't. What would some scholarship case from the projects know about holding on to pride?" He pulled the key from the ignition. He hated how she could do this to him, make him feel like he both needed to slay any dragon that came her way and throttle her himself. He never lost his cool, never let emotions rule his actions, but Lily Harris knew exactly which strings to pull to make him crazy. "Don't push me right now, Lily. Never show all your cards before you know what game you are playing."

He climbed out of the car, slamming his door to release some of his ire. She was the most frustrating woman he'd ever known. Anyone else would be grateful. But then if she were anyone else he wouldn't have bothered.

If Jake were so sure she needed her privacy now, why wouldn't he leave her alone? Lily hated the fuzzy blur of emotions that swirled about her and had for the last three weeks. Pancreatic cancer had snuck into her life so quickly, turning everything upside down and backwards until she barely knew how to stand up straight.

Every day of those last days with her father she'd had to see Jake Tolliver. Though he'd been a partner in her father's architecture firm for the last two years, she'd avoided him with the skill of a tax evader. Jake attended every party given at the house, showed up to most events she went to with her father. Even with familiarity, she'd never grown accustomed to his dangerous demeanor.

"You're being silly," her father had said when she told him she didn't trust Jake. "He is absolutely brilliant, Lily. I've never known someone so intelligent and talented at the same time. He works harder than three men together. Honestly, there is no one I trust more."

Whenever she tried to explain her aversion she was treated to another ode to Jake. She'd heard everything about him, everything he wanted people to know at least. The generous charity donations, completing jobs others deemed impossible, making deals no one could believe.

None of it could make up for the raw power than emanated from him. Such sharp predatory focus barely contained beneath a patina of sophistication. She saw the utter ruthlessness every time she looked into his dark eyes. One day he would pounce.

She never understood what Jake wanted with her father's architecture firm. He had his own, one with projects spanning the globe and partnerships in every facet of the business from manufacturing to construction. He may have started at the base of the ladder, but now he had to branch out to keep growing higher.

He'd appeared from the shadows, making her father an offer that the older man had thought was in his favor. Her father had thought himself lucky to get to work with Jake Tolliver. What a joke. The firm it took generations to build had become Tolliver-Harris, yet another arm of the Tolliver Enterprises empire. Now that legacy was gone, swallowed up by the yawning maw of debt just as the house was. Her father's attorney had warned her even that might not be enough to cover all the debts and she'd likely need to earn more.

Though she was twenty-four, holding a job had never made it to Lily's to-do list. Her father always had somewhere he needed her to be without notice, making it difficult to keep up with her classes at the university, let alone a job. She was still working on her master's thesis, but now that seemed terribly impractical. What she needed was a business degree and tangible skills, not a plethora of knowledge of the works of Jane Austen.

She needed to find a way to support herself now. She'd put off trying to figure out how while her father had been ill, but now she needed to face the difficult situation head-on. Tomorrow. She'd had enough today.

Tomorrow she would think of a way to remember her father without all the indiscretions he'd admitted to. He'd apologized profusely for the risky investments and the women, all things Lily had never realized were part of his life. She'd forgiven him everything, because really, what good would it do to blame a dying man for mistakes that were hers as well? She should have finished her degree by now. Then she might be able to find a teaching position somewhere. Or she could have chosen a more practical course of study. She'd never expected her father to take care of her forever, but she also hadn't expected her world to blow up like an atom bomb.

Jake's smug attitude proved he had known it would. Maybe that's what she'd sensed all along. He'd known about her father's issues, probably used them to his advantage to take control of the firm. If he were truly her father's friend he would have told her, would have helped her get her father the help he needed before things were so far gone no one could rectify the situation. Instead, he'd lain in wait, tearing it all to pieces like a marauder.

Lily gazed out the window of the car, her eyes growing heavy as she took in the brick façade of the home she loved. Both her parents had died within its walls, and too soon she'd have to leave her memories of them there. She prayed selling it would be enough to cover the debts. Still, she'd never get enough money to make up for what the home was worth to her.

The car door swung open, startling her from her trance. She'd been doing that too much lately, her mind never staying clear enough for her to move forward without getting stuck in the past.

"It's a beautiful home, Lily. I know you love it."

She climbed from the car and shrugged. "I've known nothing else. Soon enough it will be gone too. Gone to me at least."

"If that's what you want," he said, as if she had any choice in the matter.

Lily followed him up the stone steps, steps she'd wait on every day as a little girl for her father to come home from work. "I would keep the house if I could. There are so many good memories here."

"Memories live in your heart, Lily, not in a house." He slid a key she didn't know he had into the lock and opened the door.

"How would you know what lives in the heart? Do you even have one?" He must not, or he wouldn't be taunting her about the house today of all days.

"You think I'm heartless, Angel?" He held the door open for her, a wicked grin playing on his handsome face.

"Honestly, I never think of you at all." Lily stepped past him, wishing he would go away. In the foyer she shrugged out of her coat and laid it on the upholstered bench she'd sat on her whole life when putting on her shoes.

"You really wish that were true, don't you?"

She turned to face him, the corner of his mouth quivering as if he were trying not to laugh at her. That did it. "What I wish is for—"

"Lily, you're home."

She spun around at the sound of the warm voice, watching another of her home's fixtures walk toward her. Emmaline had a kind smile and a helmet of gray curls. She'd come to the family as a baby nurse for Lily and had never left. And now Emmaline was another thing Lily couldn't afford to keep with her.

The older woman's eyes were reddened, her lips quivering. Lily went to her instinctively and held her close. She needed to be near someone who understood what she'd lost wasn't a game, but an entire life. Her eyes grew heavy, tears prickling her lids. She needed to cry, but didn't dare let a tear fall while Jake was in the house.

"Emmaline, will you bring some coffee into the den and a sandwich for Lily." Jake said impatiently. "I don't

19

think she's eaten today."

Lily turned back to Jake, her fingers itching to slap him. Couldn't he see she wanted to be left alone? That Emmaline was grieving and didn't need to be fetching him anything?

"Of course, Mr. Tolliver." Emmaline smiled at him as she always did. For some reason she'd taken a liking to Jake from the first. Lily waited until they were alone again before speaking.

"What I eat is none of your business. And you have no right to be ordering Emmaline about. Especially today. She hates funerals or she would have been there today. And I have no intention of going into the den."

The den had been her father's sanctuary. Part home office, part study, and generally his favorite place to be. Lily hadn't gone in there since he passed.

"There are things we need to discuss alone."

"I don't want to be alone with you. Besides, I trust Emmaline completely."

"As do I. But there are things she doesn't need to know, things you may not want her to." He stepped closer to her, his expression growing hard and foreboding. Lily's breath caught in her throat and she fought the urge to back up. Enough people gave in to him. She wouldn't be another. He shook his head and walked past her, down the hall and into the den, leaving her the choice to follow or not.

As if she had any choice at all.

Chapter Two

Jake stood, looking out the window, the late afternoon sunlight softening the hard planes of his handsome face. Other women must see him like this. She tried to never think of him as a man, preferring to see him as raw power and driving determination. If she allowed herself to see him as anything more she might fall prey to him the way other women did.

He'd never brought any of them to the house, but she'd read more than enough in the papers. He had a penchant for famous and successful women. Actresses, activists and businesswomen who showcased the same polished perfection he did. He never stayed long with any of them, but they never seemed to completely disappear from his life either. It was as if once they fell for him, they never quite managed to get up.

Lily understood how that might happen. Every time his diamond-hard eyes were trained on her she felt an edgy sensation like her clothes had been stripped off and she was completely bare to him. He looked at her like he knew secrets she didn't even know she held.

He was dangerous, not to be trusted. Like all illicit

things, knowing better only seemed to deepen her fascination. But Lily would leave well enough alone and keep her distance from a man who always got what he wanted, no matter who it hurt.

Jake turned, his expression completely unreadable. "You're pale, Lily. You need to eat something. You can't afford to lose any more weight."

"I can't *afford* much of anything, now can I?" Her voice rose too high and thin to even show a semblance of control.

Jake didn't so much as blink. "Then you best eat now, don't you think?"

As if on cue, Emmaline came through the door carrying a tray of coffee and food and set it on the walnut coffee table. She didn't stay, probably to avoid the palpable tension in the room.

Lily sank onto the leather sofa, knowing she should eat but not wanting to. It was petty and childish, but she didn't want to set a precedent and do what he told her. She should be grateful for all he'd done in the last few weeks and for helping her escape today, but no amount of guilt could make her act on what she knew she should feel. Too wrapped up in grief's dark embrace, her emotions were a tangle she couldn't begin to comb out today.

"I'm not talking until you eat something." Jake turned his back to her, perusing the wall of bookshelves teeming with volumes her father had collected. Lily's chest tightened at the realization she wouldn't be able to keep any of them either.

"Promise? Because if you won't be talking, there's no point in you staying here. I doubt there's anything you'll say that Daddy didn't tell me. He was very up front with how things would be once he was gone."

"Was he, Angel? I doubt that," Jake said without turning or showing any reaction to her bitter tone. "Eat something. This is the last time I ask nicely."

"What do you know about being nice?" Her voice nearly broke as she hurled the words at him. "Why do you insist on rubbing it in that I have nothing? I'm aware. Why are you pushing me? I buried my father today. Can't you leave me alone?"

Her voice grew higher and tighter until finally it broke in anguish. She turned her face into her shoulder as her determination to stay strong dissolved under the weight of unshed tears. Her throat thickened, her world darkened as the dam burst and the stress of the day pummeled her.

It was all too much. She didn't even have it in her to resist as Jake slid next to her on the couch and gathered her in his arms. Turning to him for comfort was absurd, but there hadn't been anyone who'd gotten this close to her since she'd learned of her father's diagnosis. She'd wanted to be held each time she'd been kicked on the way to rock bottom. But there'd been no one to turn to, no one to ease the burden.

Her friends at the university never understood her relationship with her father and her society friends were concerned her father's scandal might somehow rub off on them. A month ago she'd been surrounded by people. She'd never imagined she could feel this abandoned.

The overflow of emotions poured out of her, sobs racking her body until she was truly spent. Her head pounded from crying. Her throat was tight and raw. The sensations pulled her back from the abyss to find Jake pressing his handkerchief into her hand. She sat up with a jolt, reality hitting like a slap.

The front of his shirt was wet where he'd held her. She covered her face with the cool linen, not wanting to think about how she must look—childish, weak, incapable of taking care of herself. She swallowed hard and wiped her face.

"I'm sorry I broke down. I don't—"

"You have nothing to be sorry for. You're grieving, Angel. You've lost a lot. It's normal to mourn." He reached out, tucking a lock of blonde hair behind her ear.

With one arm still around her, and a touch so gentle, she nearly believed he was a different person. Part of her wanted to get up and run, but another part needed for someone else to be strong for a moment, for someone else to hold the world on their shoulders until she could manage on her own again.

"How old were you when your mother died, Lily?"

"Four." She bit the inside of her lip to keep the tears from returning.

"That's why feeling like this is such a surprise to you. You don't remember what it's like to lose someone with so little warning. Even when you know it's inevitable, it's still devastating to lose a parent."

"You sound like you know."

He nodded in response and her stomach did a funny somersault as he began to speak.

"My mother went slowly, but it still came as a shock."

"How old were you?"

"Twenty-one. Just finishing up undergrad. It made me realize how short life could be. She wasn't even forty. Half the things she'd wanted to do with her life she never got around to. When she died I knew I wouldn't live that way. If I wanted something, I would get it as quickly as possible." He turned his intent gaze on her but she looked away, focusing on the sunset outside the window.

"And your father?"

"I wish he were dead. He never made life easy for either of us, drinking every dime she ever made."

"I'm sorry." Her hand inched toward him involuntarily. She caught the movement before she did something truly stupid like try to hold his hand.

"Why should you be? I don't need your pity, especially now. I've almost forgotten what it was like to feel that way. I think the stress of the day must have gotten to us both. Usually, I'm put off by crying."

He released her and stood, walked to the coffee table and poured himself a cup.

"I didn't ask for you to watch me."

"Of course not." He poured cream into the cup and then added a spoon of sugar. It wasn't until he handed it to her that Lily realized he knew how she took her coffee. "I liked your father. Despite his indiscretions, he was a good man and my partner. Because of that I am accountable for you. If you won't eat, at least drink the coffee. Then we can discuss what I came here for."

Lily took a sweet sip. "I can't imagine what we'd talk about."

"We've talked more today than we have in the entire time I've known you. Perhaps we're setting a precedent."

"There is nothing to say that hasn't been said." She set her cup on the table.

"We need to talk about what you plan to do now, Lily."

Closing her eyes, she drew in a fortifying breath. It wasn't his business, but he'd never let it rest until she told him. Lily looked up at him, stretching her lips into what she hoped looked like a smile. "You don't have to worry about me, no matter how *accountable* you feel. I'm not a child. When the house sells I'll get a job and then find an apartment in town. If the debts aren't settled, I'll work out a payment plan."

Jake leaned against the mahogany desk, his gaze set firmly on her. His lips twisted into a grin. "And?"

"This may be a joke to you, but it's what I'm left with. I'm doing the best I can."

"Considering you're completely unprepared to take care of yourself."

She bristled more at his condescending tone than his patronizing words. "Pardon *me* if I didn't plan on having my father's tiredness turn out to be pancreatic cancer.

Excuse *me* for not working his hidden gambling addiction into a tidy schedule. Forgive *me* for never guessing he liked to spend money on women who—"

"Stop it, Lily. I'm not in the mood for theatrics. They don't suit you."

"You're expecting me to justify myself to you, and when I do you belittle me."

"I don't mean to. I'm merely trying to show you where you stand in the world."

"Thanks so much for your concern." She laid the sarcasm in her voice as heavy as motor oil. "But I've seen the papers lately. I know what they say."

"That will go away quickly. The stories were only picked up because of your father's connection to me. The debts have been paid so they'll move on to the next scandal."

She'd never once heard him tell a joke, but he must be kidding. "How did the debts disappear? His portion of the firm and the house weren't likely to cover it."

Jake sank into the leather armchair, stretching his long legs in front of him as if he owned the place. "Do you remember last week when I spent the afternoon with your father? Taylor came too, the lawyer you were with today at the service?"

Lily could barely nod as a chill snaked down her spine. She reached the arm of the couch, needing something to ground her.

"Your father and I worked everything out so he could go in peace, knowing you were taken care of and all his mistakes wouldn't fall on your shoulders."

His words should have soothed her, let her know her father had passed in peace, but there was something more coming. The air seemed to be sucked away, like the water on the shore before a tsunami.

"He asked me to buy him out. All of his creditors have been taken care of."

"But his share of the business wasn't worth enough to cover everything."

"I also bought the house."

Her stomach knotted, her pulse racing as she clenched her cold and damp hands. She itched to slap him. Lily rose, not caring if her legs would hold her. She couldn't sit still a minute longer.

"You took everything, everything he worked for. I knew you had an agenda the first time you came here. No one would listen. I know that's why you hate me, because I saw what you were doing. You must have known about his weaknesses, so you got in, got close and waited for the attack. Where is the glory in beating a man on his deathbed?"

Jake rose slowly from the chair and stepped toward her so his height and large frame blocked out everything else in the room. Pure rage flared on his face, his dark eyes icy pools in the middle of the fire.

"Don't do this, Lily. I won't be painted the villain so you can put your father back on his pedestal. I didn't tell him to invest in Ponzi schemes that would steal from his friends, sell him a yacht that never left the harbor, introduce him to the women."

Lily felt her face distort as his words cut deeper than any knife. She turned, but he grabbed her shoulders and forced her to face him.

"The women are what bother you, aren't they?"

She lifted her chin in defiance, but when she spoke her voice cracked in anguish. "He loved my mother."

"Yes, he did. And you look just like her. Imagine his torment, to have lost the love of your life and to have to watch her image grow up before your eyes. He talked about her as if she were still alive, her picture on his desk, in his wallet, tattooed on his heart. Loving a woman that much is what drove him to the brink."

"But why didn't he ever date? Why would he use those kinds of women?"

"To soothe the hurt. They never meant anything. He couldn't have someone in his life that did, there was no room." Jake released her and paced to the end of the room and back. "He wasn't afraid to die, Lily, just panicked to leave you. I agreed to everything he asked of me. He wanted you to stay in the house for as long as you need to."

She shook her head. "The house is yours. I'll pack my things and be gone first thing tomorrow."

Jake sighed and shrugged, obviously not caring at all what she did. "That's your choice. As you said, you can make your own decisions. But before you go, you should know he asked something else of me."

"What else could there be?"

"He wanted you to have the life he planned for you, with comfort, stability and ease. He asked me to marry you."

Jake had run this conversation through in his mind a half dozen ways, and in none of them had Lily gone white and fainted dead away. At least she hadn't hit her head on the way down. Jake gathered her in his arms and sat on the leather couch. He held her tightly for a moment, hating that she either had to be crying or unconscious to let him lay a hand on her.

He pressed his face into her cascade of pale gold hair and breathed in the sweet scent of strawberries. He'd dreamed of holding her this close, but in his dreams she'd been conscious and willing.

"Open your eyes, sleeping beauty, or I will kiss you awake."

A soft noise came from her throat as she began to stir. He laid her back against the arm of the couch and got up so he wouldn't be tempted. Her eyes fluttered open as he stood.

"What happened?" She looked about the room with glassy eyes.

"I think you decided to prove your reaction wasn't theatrics. I stand corrected. Honestly, I think it has more to do with how little you've been eating. You've lost too much weight, Lily."

She wrapped her arms around her middle as she pulled herself to sitting. "I'm fine."

"Yes, people who are fine always fall to the floor with no warning." He stepped to the desk, taking a butterscotch candy out of the bowl on top. "If you don't eat something I'll take you to the hospital and have you checked out."

"You can't do that. I told you, I'm fine."

"And I told you, fine people don't faint." He handed her the candy, but she merely eyed it.

"I had a shock."

He held his hand out flat, the golden candy on his palm. "Here, now you won't have to risk touching me."

"It's not that." She pursed her lips together and plucked the candy from his hand. Their skin never made contact. "It is hard to eat when your stomach is tied up in knots, when your mind is racing so fast everything seems like a blur."

"Starving yourself will only make that worse. If you want me to think you can take care of yourself, you need to start acting like it."

"Why are you doing this?" She pulled off the gold wrapper and popped the butterscotch into her mouth.

"As opposed to what? Turning you out into the rain and convincing Emmaline to lock the door behind you?"

She lifted her chin and met his dark gaze. "She may like you, but don't be so sure you have her completely in your pocket. I'm sure she'd sneak me crumbs from your table, oh great and powerful Oz."

"And why would you settle for crumbs when you

could be at the head of the table?" Damn if his stomach wasn't tightening. He always trusted his instincts on what to say and when to say it, but with Lily he was always out of his element. She wasn't like the straightforward women he knew, and he'd watched as she passed through a line of trust-fund brats with their pie-in-the-sky promises. How did you convince a woman to want something when you couldn't even talk to her without wanting to pull your hair out?

"Be serious. I'm sure my father's request was as much a shock to you as it was to me."

"Not really. There is a lot of sense to it." And it had been his idea in the first place.

"But we don't like each other. I appreciate you'd want to provide him reassurance, but why are you bringing it up as if it's even a possibility?"

He crossed his arms. "Why isn't it?"

Her brown eyes widened in shock. "You're actually serious."

"It makes perfect sense. I'm thirty-four and I have almost everything I want. There's more money than I'll ever spend alone and this house is too large for one person."

"I'm not getting married for room and board. That's ridiculous. I'm sure if Daddy had more time to think about it, even he'd have seen that. He'd want me to get married for the right reasons."

"Like the reasons he married your mother? Loving someone so much you can't function without them? I haven't had an easy life, and I've learned the hard way how the world works. I'm not asking you to love me. You don't need to be in love to be married. I'd like a beautiful wife to come home to, one who understands how my world works and how to keep it running smoothly. You'll have the life you're accustomed to and my name."

"I'm not going to marry you. I don't even like you."

"Why is that?" He'd always wondered what he'd done, what she'd heard that made her despise him so.

"Intuition. I knew you wanted something from us and you wouldn't stop until you had it. People like you never do."

"People like what? Uncultured, underprivileged?"

"That's not what I mean and you know it."

"Then why don't you like me?" He sat beside her, pinning her with his gaze. Maybe if he could learn the answer he could find a way around it.

"You're a predator. You take what you need, do what you have to do to get what you want. I saw that the first time you came here."

"Is that what you saw? And what did I have in my sights, Lily?" He stared at her, both loving and hating that she'd known he wanted her from the first. She was so much more than the demure virgin, the haughty debutant others painted her as. He couldn't wait for the world to see what he saw.

She looked away, toying with the hem of her black dress. "I don't know why we are even talking about this. You have a girlfriend. I doubt fashion designers take to kindly to having their boyfriends propose marriage to other women, even as a perverted business arrangement."

"Are you worried about Dee?" He couldn't help but smile at her imagination. "You don't need to worry yourself about my latest mistress. They do tend to take care of themselves. And besides, that has nothing to do with you."

"You're right it doesn't." Lily stood and squared her shoulders. "I have no intention of marrying you, so what you do with your recreational sex life is your business."

This was more of a reaction from her than he'd ever had before. He'd waited years for something to give, but it always wound up being him. He couldn't help but take advantage of her jealousy. "Don't worry, Angel. I'll always make time for you."

Lily pressed her hands to her temples. "Why can't this all be a bad dream?"

"Because this is life, not something you wake up from because it's not going as you planned. This is exactly why your father wanted me to take care of you. You aren't prepared to deal with the real world, with how you'll be treated now that you don't have the upper hand. Even your plans for what to do next lack common sense. You have a degree, but the only thing it prepared you for was graduate school. You say you'll get a job, but where and doing what?"

"I don't know, all right? Taking care of my father has been my priority. I'll think about everything else tomorrow."

His mouth twisted with exasperation. "Okay, Scarlet. This is life, not one of those novels you study. If you do beg a job off someone it won't pay enough for an apartment the size of your closet. If you ask for a job as a favor there are men who will expect more in return than you are willing to give."

"And how is that any different from what you're doing?"

"If that was all I wanted I would have had you a year ago." He took a deep breath, trying to keep from screaming at her. "Is your virginity a commodity you're putting on the market?"

Lily gasped. "You don't know what you're talking about."

"Oh, but I do, Angel. What was it you told one of the other baubles at the symphony? Sex makes casual relationships too complicated. If you don't sleep with them it's easy to let them go."

Her eyes widened. "You were eavesdropping?"

"I wasn't the only one. All of those idiots you date think you quite the challenge. Most of them are fortune hunters, so they likely won't bother now, unless it's out of sport."

"Not all men are like you."

"This is not a game I'm playing. I could lie to you, could have gone about this an entirely different way and likely had you beneath me tonight. But you've been lied to and sheltered for too long. Our marriage will be an honest one. I want it to start that way from the first."

"We will *not* be getting married. You accused me of acting the heroine of a novel, but you're the one treating me like some Regency-era spinster who'll marry anyone willing to do without a dowry. I may not have many options, but I don't have to marry you. Besides, if I'm as stupid and delusional as you're saying, you really could do better."

"You're not stupid, Lily. Just overprotected and unaware that wolves dress in sheep's clothing. I can protect you from that."

She forced a laugh. "Imagine, the big bad wolf scaring off all the others before leading the lamb to the slaughter. I'm sure you meant well when you made your promise to my father, but you don't need to make any sacrifices on my account."

"It's no sacrifice. I've always planned on marrying you. When I told your father that last year he wasn't encouraging. You were dating that shipping heir, and he found him more suitable. But when he realized how little time he had left to put things right, and how poorly he'd managed everything, I became the only one he could trust to make sure you were taken care of."

Lily blinked and reached out for the leather wingback to steady herself. "But you never acted as if you liked me, let alone wanted to marry me. I don't know why you'd invent a story like this, especially after what you said about our parents' marriages."

"Love won't destroy us as it did them, Lily. Unless you are already in love with me."

"Of course not!"

"Then we have nothing to worry about. I know what I want, and I know what you need. It's the same thing."

"You have no idea what I need. It certainly isn't to be on your arm in public while everyone around us snickers about your latest conquest."

Jealousy, again. If she only knew. "No one will laugh at you, Lily. They wouldn't dare. We'll be a force, you and I. Besides, we'll be the perfect family they all envy. Especially if the children will look like you."

"Children? You've gone mad. I'm not some brood mare you can hire on for the bloodline."

"You really need to raise your opinion of yourself. You will be my wife, the mother of my children. You'll run this house and have all the social commitments you can manage. It's exactly the life you want."

"My God, you have it all worked out, don't you? You'll have this perfect façade of a family with me, and your string of mistresses to entertain you. Your life won't change—it will just wear prettier clothes."

"My life works well now, but I need more. I need you." That was it, the ultimate truth. A vulnerability he hated to admit to, much less show so plainly. What more did she need?

Lily began to shake, her breath coming in short pants. "I won't do it."

He stepped closer, lifting her trembling chin with his finger. "Would you rather I seduced you? Insulted your intelligence by tricking you the way everyone else has?

Would that be easier on you, Lily?"

"No," she said, the word barely audible.

"That's what you've been afraid of all along, that I would seduce you into things that scare you. Open you up to a world different from the dollhouse you live in. That's what you feel that you can't explain."

Lily swatted his hand away and took a faltering step backwards, reaching out for the chair again. "I don't believe you. I don't believe my father would have agreed to this."

"Don't you? I'll be honest, I think he assumed I'd never want you for more than a decoration. He never saw you as a woman, Lily. That's why he never thought to protect you."

"Stop it. I've had enough. I've had to face some harsh realities about my father, and today I had to put him in the ground." Tears spilled from her eyes as her face crumpled in a sob. She tried to speak again but couldn't rise above the emotion.

Jake lifted her into his arms, slightly surprised she didn't fight him as he carried her out of the room and up the staircase. He called for Emmaline, who appeared as he kicked open the door to Lily's bedroom.

"Help her calm down," he said to the older woman. "Then we'll need to get her something to eat." He laid Lily on her canopy bed. "You will eat before you fall asleep, or I am calling a doctor."

She turned from him, holding tightly to one of her white pillows. He wanted to say something to stop her from hurting, something to make her see she was making this harder on herself than it needed to be, something to change her mind. But he seemed to be saying everything wrong.

He had to find a way to make her see reason. If she left now she'd be far too vulnerable to protect herself. Anything that happened would be his fault.

Chapter Three

For the first time in her life, Lily Harris felt unsafe in her own home. Partly because it wasn't hers anymore, but mostly because Jake Tolliver stalked the halls. As he should since he owned them.

She set the bowl of soup on the tray Emmaline had placed on her nightstand and pulled her knees to her chest. She'd thought her life had been turned upside down when her father was diagnosed, and then again when he confessed his indiscretions. But this, his asking a man she didn't trust to marry her, was completely...insane.

Her gaze drifted to her bookshelf. While earning a degree in English literature she'd collected more than her share of historical novels. Even in Regency England, this would be odd. No doubt Jane Austen would have had fun spinning it around.

The thought lifted her spirits a little. She'd missed her first week of classes, but getting back to school and returning to work on her thesis would make her feel normal. Unfortunately, it wouldn't help her get a job or find an apartment. She didn't even know how she'd afford tuition this term.

The handle on her bedroom door clicked and turned. Jake entered without the courtesy of knocking. Lily looked down to make sure her duvet covered as much of her pink nightgown as possible before addressing him.

"If having access to my room is a condition of my staying her, I'll leave now."

"Don't make empty threats, Lily. We both know you won't leave tonight. It's late. I'm staying here too unless you object."

"Can I stop you?"

"Would you want to?" He sat on her bed, right where her feet would be if she stretched her legs out. He nodded toward the tray. "I'm glad you ate something. You've lost too much weight in the last few weeks."

"For a man with a string of girlfriends, you should know better than to discuss weight with a woman." Though the women she'd seen him with had no worries about that. He was lucky one of them hadn't speared him with a pointy hip.

"You're not taking care of yourself. Do it, or I will."

"How is it you can make food sound like a threat?" She rested her chin on her knees. "Is there anything I can take with me when I go?"

"I'd rather if you didn't. You belong in this house." His hand covered her foot. Even beneath the duvet she could feel the heat of him.

She pulled her feet closer. "I think you should go."

"What is it you think I'm going to do to you? Is your fear of me really so weak my touching you could turn everything in a different direction?" He reached for her again, this time holding her ankle through the blanket. "If it would make this easier on you, I could seduce you."

"Yes, I'm sure you could." She sat up straighter, her cheeks burning. "I've seen your list of references. If I didn't find it disgusting, I might be impressed. I'm sure your fashionista girlfriend is."

He actually laughed. "Dee Gibson is none of your concern, unless you're looking for a designer for your wedding dress."

Lily felt her jaw drop, but recovered quickly. "How sordid. Even if I needed a wedding dress, which I don't, I wouldn't have your girlfriend design it."

"You're the one who keeps bringing her up. Should I be flattered you've been so interested in my personal life?"

"I'd have to be blind not to see it."

"If it bothers you, remember today's news is tomorrow's birdcage liner. Besides, this incident with your father should teach you not to believe everything you read. Those women have something to gain by having their name connected with mine, by being being seen with me. It benefits them."

"How kind of you to pimp yourself out."

Derision and sympathy mingled in his glare. "You don't understand how the world works."

She might not be the most worldly person, but she knew women. They tripped over themselves to get to him because of who he was, yes. But it was more than the money and the handsome face. It was the vibrant power of him, the startling sexual magnetism he kept under wraps. She'd missed the full effect before tonight, always avoiding being alone with him. But now she had to face the truth. She was wary of him, not because of his brutal business acumen, but because of his ability to set her emotions on the spin cycle.

"Careful how you look at me, Lily." His grip on her ankle tightened. "If you keep that up, I might be encouraged."

"Can't you just go?"

"And leave you all alone in your white bedroom? It looks just like I thought it would. Pure. It suits you, for now."

He took everything to mean something. She'd decorated the bedroom in white when she was twenty and tired of the pink frills of her youth. It had nothing to do with virginity. She'd seen it in a design magazine and copied.

"I'm surprised you don't sleep in white." His finger traced over the collar of her nightgown.

"Sorry I didn't live up to your image of me. I'm a person who makes mistakes, not the Barbie-doll idea you have in your mind."

"It's you I've been watching. I know you better than you think. Your father thought he was doing the right thing by keeping you so protected, but it's made you so wary you don't live and you've been too sheltered to learn how."

She didn't want to hear about another thing her father had done wrong. Up until a few weeks ago, it had been the two of them against the world. Or so she'd thought. They weren't as close as she'd imagined or she wouldn't be so shocked by what her fathers' illness had uncovered. She'd devoted her life to being the best daughter she could possibly be in order to help ease the ache of losing her mother, and it hadn't helped him at all. She knew her father had doted on her for the same reasons. It seemed their best intentions only wound up hurting the other.

Lily closed eyes heavy with unshed tears and took a deep breath before opening them again. "I can't talk about him with you anymore. I'm trying to hold on to an image of the man I knew, not the one I've had to meet lately." She stared up at him, wishing he show her some mercy and go.

Jake nodded, his thumb circling her ankle. "Would it be easier if I swore you'd be happy with me?"

"You can't make me happy. I'll never forget that you took everything my father worked for. Besides, you don't want happiness, you want people to envy you."

He raised his other hand and traced his finger down her tear-stained cheek. "Actions speak louder than words anyway. I'll show you what you need. I've waited this long for you. I'll wait a little longer for you to realize all I am offering."

Lily turned her head, but his hands lifted to frame her

face and hold her still. "I'll give you everything you could ever wish for, Angel. I'll make you happy. All you have to do is let me."

Jake leaned forward, his lips brushing against hers. A small voice inside told her to fight him, to run screaming out of the room. But she was too tired to fight, and another part of her wanted to know just what she was struggling against.

He didn't press or force her, just kissed her gently as if the kiss were all he wanted. The touch was sizzling and exciting, yet wonderfully comforting. Trickles of sensation flared hotly through her body, a fire she knew he could easily stoke into a blaze.

Instead, he pulled back, staring into her eyes as his fingertips traced her forehead, eyebrows, cheeks. He leaned his head against hers, his hands still framing her face.

"Sleep well, Angel. I won't let anything hurt you." He placed a kiss on her forehead and then left her. Alone.

Lily peeked out the dining-room windows, seeing Jake already dressed for the day in his perfectly tailored suit. Beside him were half a dozen brawny men, their gazes following his direction as he pointed toward the house.

She stepped back from the window, sleepiness washing over her again. She wasn't physically tired, just emotionally exhausted. But she couldn't let fatigue keep her from speaking to Jake before he left for the day. She wanted to know when he was coming back, and she needed to put her plan in motion. In the past she'd avoided him as much as possible, but now she sought him out with equal determination.

Before drifting off last night she'd considered all he'd said. She needed a job, but as loathed as she was to admit he was right, finding one that would work around her school schedule might put her in a compromising position. She was already on a slippery slope with him, and better to dance with the devil you know.

Breakfast was laid out in the dining room just as it had been every morning for her father. Lily made herself a cup of coffee and hoped the caffeine would jumpstart her brain. To talk Jake into letting her work at Tolliver-Harris, she'd need to have her wits about her.

Jake entered the room, the warm scent of his cologne reaching out to her when he came to stand next to her as he fixed his own coffee. "I'm glad you're awake. I wanted to see you before I went back into town."

"To warn me about the goons you've hired to keep me prisoner here?" She smiled sweetly and then blew on the surface of her drink.

"They work for the construction arm of the firm. They knew your father and they want to help. I'll have two at the gate, just like last night, but during the day I thought having two more would be a good idea." His dark eyes surveyed her from head to toe, his lips quirking in a grin of approval that made her want to shiver. "It won't be for long. I'll issue an announcement today about retaining ownership of the business and everything will die down.

Without speculation, this will be old news within the week."

"So I can come and go as I need to?"

"I think you should stay in until you are stronger. You've been wearing yourself out taking care of your father, and yesterday was a shock to you. If there's anything you need, I am sure Emmaline will be happy to get it for you."

"And you accuse my father of overprotecting me." Lily shook her head. She needed to put some boundaries in place before he truly did take over her life completely. "Classes started last week, so I need to get back to school. Plus I need to find a job."

"I'll take care of whatever you need. I'll have a card issued for your expenses."

Her temperature rose. "I don't think so. I'm not interested in being a kept woman. Besides, I have tuition to pay."

"I can—"

Lily held up a hand to stop him. "I won't take your money."

"You're being ridiculous. Why should you struggle when I can afford to provide for you? You're making things so much more difficult than they need to be."

"You seem to have something wrong with your hearing. I will not take your money. I don't want to be any more indebted to you than I already am. If we can't agree on that, then I need to leave." She set down her mug with a thud and stepped toward the door. It wasn't a bluff.

Pride was all she had left.

He grabbed her arm, holding her so tightly she could feel his fingers digging into her flesh. "You aren't going anywhere until you've eaten something. If you want me to treat you like you can take care of yourself, then you damn well better start." He released her and stalked to the other end of the room.

To spite him she wanted to leave the room, but that would accomplish nothing. She still hadn't told him about her plan, and if she left now she'd just have to make something to eat later. She grabbed a banana from the table and peeled it. As she put it in her mouth she wondered if she should be eating something so blatantly phallic with Jake in the room. But then, maybe it would unsettle him the way he unnerved her.

"Are you sure you want to go back to the university?" Jake stared at her, his expression unreadable.

Lily swallowed. "Positive. I'm nearly finished with my masters and then I can teach while I work on my doctorate." She'd have her degree already if she'd applied herself. But there'd never been a rush to finish, so she'd taken the courses she wanted as they were convenient. Only three classes and a completed thesis stood in her way. She hoped to manage them all this term.

Jake merely nodded. "Then why are you looking for a job? I worked while I was in school because I had to. You don't. It's harder than you think."

"I'm not afraid of hard work."

"You don't even know what it is. This is your life,

Lily." He gestured to the ornately decorated dining room. "You live in this over-privileged world or in your books. What is it you think you can do for work? I've warned you about asking people for favors."

"Maybe I should ask you then." She pressed her hands against her legs to keep them from shaking. If he said no, she'd have to rethink everything, including school. "Surely there's something I can do at Tolliver-Harris to keep me out of harm's way?"

"Like what? It's an architecture firm, not a book club."

"You know, in order for you to get where you are, someone had to give you a chance. That's all I am asking for. If I can't make myself useful, then—"

"Then you'll marry me and stop this nonsense." A smug smile set upon his face. Threatening determination and overwhelming masculinity combined in his eyes to send a terrifying chill through her.

Lily fought back the urge to shiver, knowing she was under the scrutiny of his narrowed, probing gaze. "I want you to give me a real chance. This isn't a trap you can bait and set. I want to know the business that meant so much to my father."

Jake came to stand next to her, his cocksure grin widening. "You count on people underestimating you, don't you?" He tilted her chin, sliding his warm palm against her cheek. "Everyone thinks you're just a pretty face, a beautiful, docile decoration. I see you, Lily. I think you're getting in over your head here, but I'll make the deal if you will."

She pressed her fingernails into her palm to tamp down the anxiety. Maybe she'd overplayed her hand. But really, what choice did she have? What else did she have to bargain with? She had to succeed, because anything else would destroy her.

"If you want to learn the business I'll make sure you have every opportunity. But it's not as easy as you think. We can start you out slowly, but I won't let you answer phones and claim you learned about what the firm meant to your father." He rubbed his thumb against her cheek as if he were sweet-talking her instead of issuing ultimatums. "You'll learn every aspect of the company. If it's too much, you're free to throw in the towel at any point and focus on your thesis. And me."

Lily swallowed past the lump in her throat. This had been her idea, hadn't it? Suddenly she wasn't so sure. "It'll take a while to understand how things work."

"We'll know before year end. Besides, it'll be best if we marry before New Year's."

She blinked. "I didn't say I'd marry you. The job—"

"We're going to be married. You best get used to the idea."

"Why would you even want such a thing?"

"I told you last night. Once you've had some time to think about it, you'll see it my way."

"I won't," she barely managed to whisper. She knew that to play this game she'd at least have to agree to the terms, even if she'd rather die than follow through.

"Don't be stubborn for sport. I always get what I

want." The conviction in his voice chilled her to the bone.

"You can't have me."

His gaze slid over her body like a caress. "We both know that's not true. Tell me, Lily, do we have a deal? You can try and learn what Tolliver-Harris does, or you can plan a wedding. I know what I'd rather you do."

She lifted her chin, wanting to brush his hand free but not wanting to let him know he'd unnerved her. "I'll learn the business by the end of the year. And then I'll be free."

"You're not some caged bird. Go ahead and take some time to come to terms with wanting what you want. I have been waiting a long time, a few months more will be worth it when we ring in the New Year as man and wife." He leaned down, surprising her with a fleeting brush of his lips against hers. "One last warning before I go. I haven't lost a deal in over a decade."

He turned to go and Lily wanted nothing more than for him to finally leave her alone. But she didn't want any more surprises from him.

"Jake, will you be back tonight?"

He turned back in the doorway, a genuine smile on his face. "No, Angel. I'll stay at the penthouse during the week. The house is yours."

She watched him walk away, wondering if she'd made a bargain with the most charming devil she'd ever known.

"Lily, can you see the front gate from where you are?"

Jake turned his leather desk chair so he could look out the windows of his office, taking in the view of the rooftops in the waning light of the day.

"It's just out my window, why?"

A vision of Lily's bedroom hit him like a punch in the gut. Leaving her alone last night had been the hardest thing he'd ever done. He wanted so badly to kiss her, to truly kiss her, but he couldn't trust himself with more than a fleeting press of lips. He had to do this right. If he allowed himself more there would be no turning back, and having her regret being with him would destroy his chances.

"Where did everyone go?" Her voice faded, losing the annoyed edge she worked so hard at.

"The guards should still be there."

"Yes, but the cars beyond the gate are gone."

"I held a press conference this afternoon. Life should be back to boring as usual soon. Still, you should try not to pick up the paper or watch the news for a while."

"Why? Is there something else?"

"More of the same, but nothing you need to deal with. It will go away soon." He'd done all he could, more than he'd hoped, but still there were women excited to be in the paper, former friends angry about the money they'd lost, bored gossip-mongers masquerading as journalists who thought nothing of dreaming up lascivious scenarios. "Focus on the man you knew, not the one who can't explain himself now."

"I'm trying." The tremor in her voice cut him to the

quick.

His voice softened. "Do you need me to stay at the house with you?"

"No, you said you were staying in town."

He sighed with a combination of exasperation and relief. "I am, for now. Once we're married I'll change my schedule so I'll be home every night."

"Not to worry. I'm sure to win our deal and you'll be able to keep up your frantic pace." Her silky voice held a challenge.

"You didn't seem so averse to the idea in your bedroom last night." His deep tone simmered with barely checked passion.

She drew in a sharp breath. "It won't happen again."

"You don't sound so sure. Are you thinking about it right now?"

"Please stop." Her voice shook slightly. It was hard to spar with her when he couldn't see her face to know if she were all right or putting on an act.

"I don't want another night like last night."

"Lily, you have to be strong. If people see your weaknesses, they'll take advantage of them."

"Is that why you don't show any?"

Thank goodness she couldn't see his smile. If she only knew. "No, I don't have any. Makes it much easier to make bargains with pretty girls."

"Ha. I'll be fine as long as you'll be fair."

"I'm always fair."

She scoffed. "Your ruthlessness is legendary."

"All the more reason why I'll be supervising your training personally. You'll learn who I am for yourself rather than relying on what you read in the papers or overhear at society events."

"You don't have time to babysit me. Besides, I'll just be in one of the departments, billing or something."

"No, you want to learn your father's business, you'll learn each part of it. And then you'll find out how the different parts work together. Be glad you're learning about a single architectural firm. If you'd wanted to study my business it would take much longer than three months."

"Jake Tolliver, the great and powerful." Sarcasm laced her words.

"Lucky for you. If not, you'd still be mired in scandal."

"I never asked for you to do anything." He could almost hear her mind downshifting into its well-bred, polite mode. "It's all been your choice. I am grateful, but—"

"Not grateful enough to marry beneath you."

She sighed. "I never said that. My idea of marriage and yours is very different."

"Your idea comes from those ancient novels you study. Mine is current and realistic. As you learn more about the world, you'll see everything differently."

"If marrying you is current and realistic, may I never learn anything beyond the idealistic and old-fashioned.

There is more to life than money and social standing. Maybe someday you'll learn *that*."

The click of the phone call ending echoed in his ear. He hated that she hung up on him, but couldn't help but be relieved that her chutzpah showed she was ready to start living again.

Chapter Four

It took a week for Lily to arrange things with her professors and settle on a work schedule. Thankfully, Jake did as he promised and stayed in town, giving her time to catch up on her schoolwork and get her bearings again.

When she'd last seen him she'd been so out of sorts, caught in the eye of the storm of grief. She still missed her father terribly, but having taken the time to reflect and center herself again, she was confident she wouldn't react to Jake so easily. She knew she owed him a debt of gratitude for the mountains he'd moved to bury her father's scandals. She owed him more because without his interventions the sheer misery of the situation she'd been left might have consumed her and driven her to things she dared not even think of.

Jake had helped her, and though she knew what he expected in return, she had no intention of giving in to his demands. Learning a business she knew little about in less than three months might be impossible, but so was the alternative.

Tolliver-Harris had been her father's biggest

accomplishment, and it would be her salvation. She'd been in the mirrored glass high-rise office building hundreds of times, but never had she been so acutely aware that she had no idea what actually happened there as she was when she reported for her first day. Anxiety niggled at her, but she was a pro at keeping her fears hidden.

Still, she couldn't help but wish she'd paid more attention when her father talked about the business, or that she'd thought to get a job before. She might have even worked here, which would mean she'd have tangible skills and wouldn't need to be playing this cat and mouse game with Jake, a lion if ever there was one.

Taking a deep breath scented with the astringent lemon cleaner ever present in the office, she stepped to the reception desk. Before she could eek out so much as a "hello" Jake appeared, taking her by the arm and giving her the world's fastest tour of all seven floors. She knew he owned the entire building, his own holdings taking up the other twelve stories.

He moved her through everything so quickly her mind was a whirl with names and titles, many of the faces already familiar. She'd been coming to the office since she was a little girl, so warm greetings came as no surprise, nor did the thinly veiled pity in the eyes of the other employees. Everyone knew about the scandalous stories. They probably knew more than she did, and had for much longer.

Lily tried not to think about it as Jake settled her in the Human Resources department. She wanted to demonstrate she wasn't the simpering bride he thought he wanted, but more than anything she needed to prove to herself she could take care of her own needs. Allowing Jake to take over where her father had left off might be the path of least resistance, but she'd learned the hard way a road like that could lead you right off a cliff.

The morning in HR went smoothly. She learned how to fill out her own forms, then how they were processed and filed. The clerk apologized for having her organize the files, but Lily loved the rote brainlessness of the activity. She was just finishing up the filing backlog when Jake appeared.

Lily tried not to look at him, wishing he would leave her alone, but she couldn't help noticing how the women in the department reacted to him. They looked at him almost as if he were royalty. She wondered if they observed the sinuous grace when he moved, how something as simple as walking into a room highlighted the power held under exacting restraint.

"Lily, come with me." He held out a hand.

She didn't know whether he meant to keep hold of her, so she let her gaze flick up and away as she joined him. He didn't say another word until they were in the elevator.

"It's time for lunch." He stabbed at the button for the lobby.

"Oh, I hadn't realized." She checked her watch, surprised to see how much time had passed. "Since I am only here three days a week, I shouldn't take a break. I need to put in as much time as possible."

"You still need to eat. We're going to lunch."

She shook her head. "Funny, I don't recall you asking."

Jake turned to face her in the empty elevator, making her take an involuntary step back. She hadn't realized just how big he was, or how small the lift was, or how close he'd come to stand until he turned his gaze on her. The corners of his sensuous lips twitched into a taunting grin.

"Miss Lilianna Harris, will you do me the honor of allowing me to accompany you to lunch? That's how they ask in your fairy tales, isn't it?"

Oh, and he'd been doing so well. "I don't study fairy tales. I've found enough ogres and trolls in real life lately." She gave him a pointed look. "I study Victorian-era English novelists. Pre-Victorian, really. Jane Austen's time was a bit before what typically comes under the Victorian umbrella. But yes, I suppose they'd approve of your attempt at manners and decorum."

"You really are from another time. Those flighty girls you hang around with at parties can barely string a sentence together, and yet you can probably give a lecture on Pre-Victorian whatever, right now."

Her instinct was to tell him the debutants she knew weren't flighty, but she hadn't heard boo from any of them since whispers of her father's activities had begun to swirl. Her father had encouraged many of his friends to make investments that turned out to be fraudulent, so it was almost understandable that their daughters would be upset. Almost. The people she had classes with weren't much better, though with them she expected it had more to do with not knowing what to say, rather than not wanting to be sullied by association.

She'd always kept her life compartmentalized, kept her relationships in the realm they belonged so as not to have any awkwardness. Now, when she could have used a few close friends, she found she had a plethora of acquaintances and no one who cared enough to look deeper than the surface to make sure she was okay.

"Why are you looking at me like that?"

Lily blinked, not realizing she had been. "Like what?"

"Like an object to be studied. You're not usually so blatant about admiring me."

She startled at the idea of admiring him, too caught off-guard to refute it. "I was merely thinking the debs probably can't form a sentence because they're plotting ways to spend your money. It's how they think of men. A bank balance like yours probably boggles their minds."

"Too bad you're not so easily impressed. Imagine if what pleased me pleased you." A wicked grin lit his face. "Though I am sure in some ways what pleases you will be my pleasure. Don't you think so?" The bell rang and the doors slid open. Jake stepped out first and Lily followed. She kept her eyes on the marble tiles of the floor, begging her heated cheeks to stop flaming.

She didn't understand how he could have such issues with his humble beginnings when he had such arrogance about everything else. Especially his obvious prowess with women. Besides the magazine articles she'd seen, she'd witnessed the way women reacted when they met him. Every time she'd ever been forced to make introductions, she'd also had to confirm a rundown of his assets and availability.

None of that had entered her mind the first time she'd been introduced to him at a dinner party at the house. Her father had called her over to meet a colleague as he often did. Nothing seemed out of the ordinary until she'd found Jake Tolliver's shrewd gaze trained on her.

She'd managed to keep her voice smooth and calm as they were introduced, but beneath the façade every fight-or-flight response her body possessed had gone off full tilt. The shadow of unease had darkened as he'd taken her hand and lifted it to his lips. Her heartbeat had accelerated at the teasing glimmer in his dark eyes.

She'd tried to look away, but only found herself noticing every detail of his charcoal gray suit and how it fit his lean, tanned body to precision. Listening to the sensual tone of his voice had her looking at him again. He'd said only that he was glad to meet her, but the way his gaze had boldly raked over her body, coupled with his enigmatic expression, had caused a panic deep within. What had been a shadow of apprehension had crashed against her in a turbulent collection of thunderous clouds.

This was a man not to be overlooked. A man unlike any other she'd ever met. She immediately knew trusting him would change her forever. And so she hadn't.

"Lily? The car?"

She looked up to find they were outside, a few blocks down from the building, where his green sports car was parked alongside the curb.

Shaking her head, she put on her best smile and lied. "Just thinking about work."

"There is more to life than work." He pulled open the door for her.

"How would you know?" She slid inside.

Jake laughed as he closed the door, then rounded the car and climbed in. He started the engine and pulled out into traffic. "I meant you don't need to be so serious all the time. Always thinking. After all you've been through the last month it's important you pace yourself."

"I'm under a deadline, remember? I have to prove to you I understand the firm before New Year's." Plus she had to keep up with her classes, finish her thesis and then defend it. Deadline was an understatement.

"If it's too much for you, you can give in and plan a wedding instead of getting paper cuts while shuffling files."

"I'll take my chances with the files. They are much more appealing than being selected as a bride because of my bloodline."

Something in her response seemed to amuse him. "What makes you think that?"

"You made a business deal on my father's deathbed that included marriage. Hardly the makings of a romance."

"Why fall prey to romantic inclination? I want what you have to offer. You need what I can provide. It makes sense."

His cool, aloof manner irked her. "Not to me. I don't understand why you think I'll change my mind."

"Everyone sees it my way in time." He smiled in smug delight.

"You are the most arrogant man I've ever known."

"It takes confidence to convince people to trust you. Honestly, did you ever trust any of those simpering trust-fund brats you dated? The only depth those idiots have ever showed is to a mirror."

The heavy sarcasm in his voice annoyed her further. "Who I see is none of your concern."

A muscle clenched along his jaw. "The hell it isn't. I'm merely giving you enough rope to tangle yourself up in. We both know coming to work for Tolliver-Harris is merely a stall tactic. I'm indulging it because I think it might help build your confidence."

"You're the one tearing me down at every turn!"

"Oh Angel, if I was you'd still be drying your tears." He pulled the car alongside the curb and turned to face her. "I want you, Lily, but I don't want you broken. Winning you that way would tarnish the prize."

"If I'm so easily broken and overly serious, why do you want me at all? Why not leave me alone and select your bride from a more accommodating catalog?"

"You are the most beautiful and intriguing woman I've ever known. You're intelligent and generous and completely fascinated by everything I do. It doesn't matter if you can't see how good we'll be together, because we will be. Besides, nothing I've ever enjoyed has come easy."

The audacity of the man. She offered him a mocking smile. "Not even your fashionista girlfriend?"

He arched a brow. "Dee is certainly nothing like you. Let's stop bickering like we're already married, shall we? Besides, we've reached the restaurant."

Lily looked out the window and her stomach sank. She hadn't been to the VQ since her father fell ill. They'd come here together often and he'd always see a half dozen people he knew. Her chest tightened at the thought of seeing someone who knew her father, who might still be angry about investments gone wrong.

Jake ushered her inside quickly and they were immediately led to a table by a waiter whose attentiveness showed he obviously served Jake often. That made her wonder who else he brought here, business associates or his colorful collection of mistresses. As they made their way to the table, Lily could feel the weight of the stares on her.

Jake took her hand, keeping her close to him as they walked through the dining room. "Never look down, Lily," he whispered to her. "Face things head-on."

She didn't fight his hold on her and held her head high, though inside she wanted to run. At their table Jake stood behind her chair as she sat.

"Why are they all looking at me?" she asked.

"Who's arrogant now? They're probably wondering about me, not you."

She didn't care if he was lying to make her feel more at ease. She'd take it. "Why would they look at you when there are so many pictures in magazines. Pictures last longer."

"I beat out a few of them yesterday. I bought an apparel company."

"Clothing? You deal in restoration. I understand why you have architecture and construction firms under your umbrella, but clothing?" She spread her napkin in her lap.

"Diversification." He leaned forward and looked at her intently. "The company has a great product, it's just poorly managed. I'll fix that and sell it for a profit within a few months."

"The way you juggle companies I wonder why you deal in architecture at all."

He sat back and sighed. "Because I am a restoration architect. It's what I love to do. It's just not the only thing I'm good at."

The waiter appeared, but Jake waved off his offer of menus, instead ordering for them both. His selection sounded fabulous, but the audacity of being ordered for sat wrong with her.

"I can read a menu," she said, taking a sip of her ice water.

"You don't need to. I know all your favorites."

"I think you are just overly concerned with what I eat."

He shook his head. "I care that you take care of yourself. I don't like to see you gaunt and tired. Just like you watch me, I watch you. It's taught me to notice when you're neglecting yourself as well as what you like. I know what you move around on your plate and what you actually will eat. You love shellfish, but not fish, and you rarely bother with poultry in any form. You always finish your salad unless it has olives. You like soups but not chowders, tarts but not cake. I've never once seen you spill anything."

Lily laughed like she hadn't been able to in months. The absurdity of him studying what she ate was simply too much to hold in. Finally, she wiped her eyes and smiled at him. "Thanks, I needed that I think."

"You're beautiful when you laugh. It makes your eyes sparkle, your whole face glow."

Her cheeks prickled with heat at the compliment. She dropped her gaze, wishing he hadn't changed the tone. If things could stay simple between them she knew she could make him see reason.

"Angel, don't hide yourself from me. You'll wish you hadn't."

She looked up. "Why? Do you plan on punishing me for my insubordinate refusal to marry you?"

"No, because one day soon we will be married and you'll look back on your behavior as childish."

"You're so much older than me, it is no wonder you think so." There wasn't quite ten years between them, but she had to agree that considering the differences in how they'd lived their lives it seemed more like eons.

The waiter arrived with their food, silencing the argument. She didn't compliment him on his choice of seared prawns with green curry and a Thai-noodle salad for her. She ate it, and he'd have to take that as praise enough.

Conversation over lunch stayed strictly on business. He filled her in on a few of the bigger projects, including one her father had been working on before he became ill. Jake had won a contract to modernize a long-closed hotel. He talked of how he and her father had worked together, brainstorming ideas for the venture. Having someone focus on the good things her father did brought her a comfort she'd been missing. The charities her father supported had all ignored his passing. Usually generous contributors were acknowledged upon their death. She hated how all his good work had been erased by latent indiscretions.

When their plates were cleared and the *Gianduja*-praline truffle tart brought to the table with two forks, Lily finally felt comfortable in Jake's presence. Until she saw the woman stalking toward their table.

Dee Gibson was instantly recognizable with her flowing red hair and perfectly tailored dress, no doubt one of her own designs. Her persona was chronicled in magazines thanks to her stint on a television reality show. Lily would have to be blind not to know who she was, or what she was to Jake Tolliver.

"Here you are," Dee exclaimed, sliding a fuchsia talon-manicured hand onto Jake's shoulder and giving it a squeeze. "I called the office and they told me where to find you."

Jake looked up at her, his expression uninviting. "I thought you were busy."

Lily's stomach clenched. She didn't care to witness Jake and his lover having any kind of conversation. This was exactly what she'd been trying to point out to him. Women did not share men, no matter what men found attractive.

"The meeting wrapped quickly," Dee said. "I thought I'd breeze by since I had to cancel lunch. Not to worry though, I'll make it up to you tonight." She gave his shoulder a squeeze.

Lily let her fork clatter to the plate, the desert no longer appealing. In fact, she'd be lucky if her lunch didn't repeat on her. Still, Dee was key to making Jake see reason about his marriage delusions.

"I assumed you'd still be busy tonight. I was about to ask Lily to join me at the fundraiser. She's well acquainted with the charity set."

Dee looked Lily over from top to bottom and then turned back to Jake, clearly unthreatened. "Don't be silly. You know I'd rather be with you than negotiating. After all, that's what I have lawyers for. Isn't that what you're always telling me?"

"If you insist." He motioned for the waiter to bring

another chair and then ordered coffee for Dee and himself. "Lily, would you like milk to drink?"

"I'm fine." She bit back the urge to ask why he didn't already know since he claimed to know her so well. She needed to stay calm and let Dee stake her claim on Jake. If Dee demanded his loyalty, it would be that much harder for him to push the ridiculous marriage issue.

"Milk?" Dee laughed as she settled into her seat. "How old are you, honey?"

"Lily doesn't drink coffee after noon. She doesn't keep our hours. Actually, I don't believe the two of you have met." He introduced them and then leaned back in his chair, also leaving the delectable dessert untouched.

"Oh, now I understand." Dee flipped her sheet of red hair over her shoulder and turned her intent gaze on Lily, a bitter and dangerous glint in her eyes. "Such a shame about your father. I hope you're getting over the shock of everything. The media has been ruthless."

"I wouldn't know," Lily smiled, unable to acquiesce since her father had been brought into the mix. "Jake has made sure I haven't had to deal with any of it. Besides, there's nothing more for them to dig up. The whole thing has blown over rather quickly."

"I'm sure Jake quieted things the best he could, but the sordid mess is sure to keep coming back. Like a bad penny, I think they say."

Jake cleared his throat. "Maybe I should quiet you, Dee. Lily's father just died. I think we can let her deal with that without bringing up rumor and conjecture."

"Of course. I'm sorry, honey. Isn't it wonderful your father had such a caring partner willing to look after you?" She rubbed her hand on Jake's arm.

Staying calm grew harder. Lily didn't know if this woman was trying to provoke her or simply had the social graces of a cow. Perhaps Dee knew of Jake's plan. Maybe they'd even discussed how things would work. Either way, disrespecting her father and belittling her wasn't the way for Dee to make nice. Lily reminded herself that they both wanted the same thing, for Dee to be the one with Jake so Lily could remain free. As much as she wanted to gush about Jake's proposal just to watch the woman squirm, it would accomplish nothing. Except maybe a smug sense of satisfaction.

"Jake has been very kind to me," Lily began. "He's allowed me to stay at his house, given me a job, he even makes sure I'm eating properly. Really, I couldn't ask for more."

"Of course not. Jake always takes care of his responsibilities."

The venom in the woman's voice nearly poisoned Lily's good intentions. Luckily, self-preservation ran deeper. "I try to pay him back the best I know how, looking after the house and working hard at the firm. You know, you should come to the house for dinner. Your designers' eye could really help Jake put his own stamp on the place."

Dee's eyes widened in shock. Lily hoped Dee would recover quickly from the knowledge that her lover had a young woman living in his new home. The house was gorgeous, just the bait she needed to get the other woman to start working Jake on her end.

"That's a lovely idea, Lily." Jake had a smug smirk on his face. "I think you should come out on Saturday night, Dee, since I'll be spending the weekend at the house." He winked at Lily from the side of his face hidden from Dee.

He liked it, liked watching two women clash over him. Lily began to worry she'd overestimated his fondness for Dee Gibson. Maybe he saw her as a passing fancy and expected his bride to spar with each new plaything he collected. Lily suppressed a shudder at the thought.

When the coffee was served Dee monopolized the conversation with talk of fabrics and Jake's latest acquisition. Boredom drove Lily to the tart. The chocolate and coconut cookie crust was much more interesting than the couple she sat with, the truffle filling had infinitely more depth.

By the time Dee made her exit, Lily was more than ready to get as far away from Jake as humanly possible.

"You promised to stay in town," she said through clenched teeth. "If you'll be at the house this weekend, I'll find somewhere else to be."

"But you just invited a guest. Would you rather I leave you to deal with Dee on your own, Angel? I don't think so. You're not playing a smart game with her. She has nothing to do with what happens between you and me."

"In your dreams. She saw right through your plan as well. For a man who knows so much about the world, you know nothing about women if you think she'll put up with your marriage plans."

Jake shrugged. "Then she's free to find another way to get into parties."

"And you'll just replace her with another model?" Lily huffed. "Sometimes you do go for models, don't you?"

"Jealousy does not become you."

"I'd have to care in order to be jealous. And I don't. I'll get out of your way and let the two of you have a romantic weekend at the house."

"You'll do nothing of the kind. You invited her. I'll help you deal with her, but I won't clean up the mess on my own."

Lily sank back in her chair, hating that in order for her plan to work she'd have to be privy to a Jake-and-Dee love fest. "I think I'm growing to hate you."

Jake tossed his napkin on his plate and rose. "It's a thin line between love and hate. You should be careful not to cross it, or to cross me. I want you, Lily. Don't make me lose my patience."

Chapter Five

"Finally, everything makes sense." Dee sidled next to him at the bar of the charity auction. "I was beginning to think I'd lost my touch."

Jake merely grunted and turned to face the room full of other well-dressed guests while she ordered her martini. These functions would be so much easier to get through once Lily was at his side. He clutched his glass in his hand, wishing he'd ordered a double.

"She's very pretty, younger than I expected. But then I guess that might be why it's so easy for her to manipulate you."

He swirled the ice in his glass. "Are you finished with this conversation? I'm not having it with you."

"Oh, sure you are. You've made me part of this game the two of you are playing. She thinks we're together. So do most people, but you haven't done anything to clue her in. And I know you. You have a reason."

"Lily Harris is none of your business, Dee. She's nothing like you. Don't bother trying to drag her down."

"She may think she's better than people who've worked for what they have, like us. But don't think she doesn't have designs on you. She's a spendaholic looking for a financial savior. She wants you to recreate her life for her so she can go back to being the perfect princess, complete with the castle."

Jake closed his eyes, wishing anything about Lily were as simple as Dee made it out to be. He turned his gaze on Dee, noticing how low cut her bright green dress was tonight. Usually she went conservative for the events he asked her to attend with him. Damn. If Dee had decided to make a play for him, the whole situation could get sticky.

"You don't like the dress?" She placed a hand on her hip. "You'll have to stand closer to me if you want to make the Scene and Heard column."

"Why would I want to do that?" He was here to write a check and talk to a few clients, not publicize his involvement in the charity.

"For the same reason you haven't told the princess you're my silent partner, not my lover. You want to make her jealous." Dee stepped closer, tilting her head so her hair flowed over her bare shoulder. "Whisper in my ear when you talk. It will get a picture in the paper. You want her to see us together."

"No, I don't." Jake set his glass on the bar. Lily's worries about his relationship with Dee were all in her head. He wasn't going to pander to her jealousies, but he wasn't about to feed into them either.

Dee shrugged her shoulders. "Yes, I'm sure our little dinner party this weekend will be quite cozy. I don't know what she's trying to pull, but I don't trust her. Is she trying to show you how much better she'll fit in your new life than I do?"

If only. "You don't know what you are talking about, Dee. She's gone through a lot in the last month. Cut her a break."

"If you swear to me you'll have an iron-clad pre-nup. That girl has gold digger written all over her."

He leveled his gaze at her. "You have got to be kidding."

"I wish I were. It's obvious you're taken with her. I thought it was out of some sense of duty to her father, or maybe you just like the idea that a kid from the projects could snag himself a society bride. I know I'd be tempted if someone with old money wanted to legitimize me."

"You really need to stick to creating clothes. The stories spinning in your head are unbelievable." He pressed his fingers to his forehead, trying to ease the ache building there.

"I wish it were a story. I'd make up a happy ending for you. But I don't think this has one. She wants you. I can tell by looking at her, trust me, women can see these things. And you are falling for it, and for her."

"I can take care of myself, Dee. You don't need to worry about me."

"Somebody needs to, Jake. You may work well with women in business, but if you think that girl isn't playing you, you have a lot to learn about how women get what they want."

Jake rolled his eyes. Dee used all of her assets to get what she needed, but she came from a different world than Lily did. Always reliant on status and money, Lily had never thought of herself as an asset until now. That's why he was trying so hard to be up front with her about what he wanted. He couldn't help it if Lily jumped to conclusions, especially if those assumptions made her see him as something she wanted for herself.

Lily tried to convince herself Jake bringing his mistress to the house was a good thing. Dee Gibson was attractive, successful and determined. With a little encouragement, Lily knew Dee was more than capable of twisting Jake's arm until his focus was solely on her. When he was enamored with another woman he'd leave Lily alone and she'd be free of his pursuit and proposal. It was a great solution, and she refused to think about why it made her so uncomfortable.

Lily busied herself with setting the house for guests. The idea of a designer redecorating the house pained her. She couldn't imagine the house looking any other way, so she'd made sure everything was perfect. Maybe then she wouldn't have to hear about any remodeling plans.

She'd just finished creating a festive autumn-leaves and gourd centerpiece on the dining-room table and was heading upstairs to dress when she heard the front door open.

She turned to see Jake highlighted in the entry, a playful smile on his face. Obviously he hadn't been dreading the evening the way she had. She reminded herself to remain aloof, to never let him see how each time she saw him he incited more of a reaction in her than the last.

"Have you been expecting me, Angel?" He towed a small case behind him, a bottle of wine beneath one arm and bouquet of flowers in his hand.

She shook her head. "I was just heading upstairs to change. I don't want to be unprepared when your girlfriend arrives." She turned and took a step up the stairs.

"Lily, wait." He stepped toward the stairs and caught her wrist, tugging it so she had to turn and face him.

She slanted her head in inquiry, not wanting to say anything too revealing. Something was stirring inside of her at the thought of him bringing gifts into her home to give to Dee. It was stupid and prideful. She couldn't let it show.

"I brought you these for your room. It needs some color." He held out the bouquet. She looked down at the vibrant arrangement of heart-shaped Peruvian lilies in different shades of pink, orange and white. The brilliantly colored blooms made her smile as she took them. She quickly checked the reaction. She had to stay on task or everything would be for naught.

"Good idea. If I had them out Dee might get jealous. Unless you brought something for her as well? She strikes me as the long-stemmed red rose type," Lily said, a crisp edge to her voice.

"Are we starting this already? Need I remind you this dinner was your idea? I won't have you being rude to her. You're better than that."

Lily clenched her jaw against the words she wanted to spew at him. Every syllable would make her seem jealous, and she couldn't afford to be. It was a silly reaction, and one she would contain in order to earn her freedom.

Instead, she rolled her eyes and tugged herself free of his magnetic pull. She sashayed up the stairs, well aware he watched her every move. Safely behind her bedroom door she let her guard down and gave herself a moment to wallow in the frustration of the situation. She was starting to have feelings for a man who could destroy her, who wanted her to be a puppet on a string he could yank about. Everyone would laugh behind her back and her heart would shatter at what she'd be forced to endure. Her only hope of escaping him with her pride intact was a woman who obviously couldn't stand her.

Lily rang the intercom down to Emmaline, asking for a vase for the flowers, and then set to work getting ready. Getting dressed was a chore when she remembered the snide barbs like, *"How old are you honey?"* She didn't want to look provocative and risk peaking Jake's interest, but she didn't want the fashion designer he was sleeping with offering her wardrobe tips either.

She settled on a strappy empire dress in black. The scooped neckline and crisscross straps in the back definitely made her look like a woman, but the pleated knee-length skirt kept her well covered.

A knock on the door turned her from her self-inspection. "It's open," she called to Emmaline as she made a last check of her appearance in front of the full-length mirror. "Thanks for bringing the vase up. I know you're busy."

Lily gasped as she caught Jake's reflection in her mirror. She spun around. "What are you doing in my room?"

"You said the door was open. If that's not an invitation—"

"It wasn't. I thought Emmaline was at the door." Lily turned back around, trying to look everywhere but at his reflection. "She'll be here any minute."

"With this?" He lifted the vase in his hand, catching her gaze for the first time. "You're welcome."

"Can you go now?" She didn't want him in her room again. Not after what had happened the last time.

He shook his head and took a step closer. His entire demeanor reminded her of an animal on the hunt, all lithe covertness and lethal determination.

"I need to finish getting ready." She pressed her lips into a line, trying to keep her breathing steady when she was on the verge of a panic attack.

"I have something for you." In the mirror she watched him set the vase on her vanity next to the bouquet. As he stepped closer to her, he slid a hand into his pocket.

"I don't want you to give me anything." She smoothed her damp palms against the cool fabric of the dress.

"I *want* you to have it."

He stood behind her, so close the heat of him pressed against her back and pushed the air from her lungs. She struggled to breathe, hating the way her chest heaved with a gasp.

"Relax, Lily. I'm not here to make love to you. There isn't time for that." He rubbed his hands on her bare arms and prickles of desire, fiery and heavy, ran through her body.

He removed his hands and Lily closed her eyes against the sense of loss. She couldn't do this much longer. There was something hypnotic and addictive about the man, something she was completely susceptible to. She had to get free of him soon or she'd never be able to.

Cold metal slid against her throat and she opened her eyes, watching as Jake fastened an exquisite diamond necklace about her neck. It was unlike anything she'd ever seen, a sweeping design of curls and loops in a wistful and feminine pattern. The design incorporated sparkling baguettes surrounding shining round stones and dripping with pear-shaped diamonds. Her hand lifted to touch it of its own accord.

She had lots of jewelry from her father and even some from her mother. She'd never put much thought into it, but those pieces were either classic or suddenly seemed very simple, nothing as exquisite and modern as this.

"I'm glad you like it. I knew you would."

"I can't," she said, the words barely audible. He'd draped her in thousands of dollars of diamonds, an exquisitely beautiful collar to choke her with.

"I insist. I saw it and knew it was made for you."

"But it wasn't. And you shouldn't buy me things."

He wrapped an arm around her waist and leaned his head against hers, their gaze meeting in the mirror. His eyes gleamed like glassy obsidian and in that moment she saw the future he dreamed of. They did make a striking couple, his strong, dark features a compliment to her soft, light countenance.

"Then don't think of it as for you. It's for me. So I can watch you tonight and know you are wearing the necklace I gave you."

"But it must cost a fortune."

"I can afford it. And more. When I see something that suits you I'll buy it, and I want you to accept it without objection."

"You want me to thank you for it." A vision of just how he likely expected to be thanked flashed in her mind. It thrilled her even more than the jewels around her neck.

He kissed her temple. "It made you happy for a second before you overthought it. That's all I wanted."

She believed him for a moment, believing maybe there was more to him then she'd ever fathomed. But just as quickly as that thought came to mind, so did the realization they would not be alone for dinner.

"Did you buy this to spite Dee?" Her stomach twisted,

her skin cooling as a shiver crept into her bones. She was so outmatched in these games.

"Oh, Lily." Jake chuckled and released her, stepping back. "You really know how to ruin a moment." He turned and left her room, closing her door behind him.

She let out the breath she was holding and met her own gaze in the mirror. Her eyes widened at the changes she saw there. The dress was the same and the necklace had nothing to do with it. Her eyes shone, her flushed skin providing a glow that hadn't been there before. When she'd seen herself earlier she'd been teetering on the edge between latent adolescence and womanhood. Now there was no doubt she'd crossed the threshold. Her heart squeezed knowing Jake Tolliver had made it happen.

Dee Gibson was absolutely stunning. It was more than the off-the-shoulder silk dress in exactly the same blue as her eyes, more than the soft waves of red hair, more than the way she knew how to move so every curve of her body was on display without showing anything. She epitomized everything Jake needed in a wife.

The observation should have made Lily happy. She had prepared herself for being outshone, had planned on it, but watching the comfortable way they spoke to one another made her stomach feel as if it were lined with lead.

Through dinner she played with her food, unable to eat anything while watching the spectacle. Dee had come to show Jake how compatible they were, how much better she fit in his life. And she did it brilliantly from the astute talk of business to the flirtatious energy of their interaction. It was exactly what Lily needed, but it felt like the opposite.

Watching them together filled her brain with all kinds of snarky remarks. Yet she couldn't comment on the flirting and the flattery. She needed it, needed Dee to spin her web of seduction so tightly Jake couldn't help but be caught up in it.

"Lily's necklace is certainly different." Dee's words pulled Lily into the conversation she'd been intent on avoiding. "A bit more whimsical than what I like to design, but it makes use of shapes like I'm thinking of doing."

"You should stick with clothing and shoes. You don't want to diversify too widely. If you need to expand quickly you'll have to bring in other investors and you hate to have to answer to anyone."

"Oh honey, I know someone willing to give me whatever I need." Her voice was smooth and seductive and made Lily want to tell her exactly who had bought the necklace she was admiring.

Made her want to mention how he'd fastened it against her throat, how he'd kissed her last week. A small part of her wanted to test him right now and see whose bidding he was willing to do. Her back tightened as she realized just what she was doing. She was justifying her jealousy, trying to see if, when it came down to it, he'd choose the mistress or the fiancée. Not that she was.

"Where did you get the necklace, Lily? It looks real.

Maybe I'll look into carrying the line in my boutiques."

She knew how she wanted to answer, but didn't trust herself to hold the cattiness in. Instead she stalled for time by taking a long drink of the fruity red wine Jake had brought.

"It looks real because it is. I bought it for her." Jake cast Lily a disapproving glance. Her heart sank. He *had* bought it to make Dee jealous.

"Honey, really. Why would you embarrass her like that?" Dee's saccharine smile did nothing to sweeten her sour tone.

"Embarrass her?"

"You can't say no when a man gives you a gift that expensive."

Lily swallowed hard, recognizing the double meaning. She hadn't denied the gift, and now it would be assumed she wouldn't deny Jake. Even with as beautiful as the necklace was, she should have ripped it from her neck and tossed it back at him. And now she couldn't hold her tongue, couldn't let him think she agreed.

"Jake has been very kind to me, looking after me now that my father is gone."

"Of course he has." The bitter edge to Dee's tone sliced like a blade. "His partner's young daughter is lost and vulnerable, all alone in the world. What she needs is to live in his house, work at his company and wear his diamonds. Don't you think?"

Lily was torn between tossing what was left of her wine in the cow's face or starting to cry at how right she was.

"Dee, really. You shouldn't talk about things you know nothing about." A rough thread of warning wove through his voice.

Lily looked up at Jake's defense of her. Instead of a sympathetic gaze she found nothing but the dark, cold stare that had been chilling her to the bone for the last two years.

Lily closed her bedroom door behind her and slumped against it, flipping the lock with a flick of her wrist. When she was alone with Jake Tolliver, sometimes she forgot who he was. Lucky for her, he had no problem showing his true colors.

He was a perfect match for the hard edges and biting remarks of Dee Gibson. They deserved each other. So why was she shaking because she'd caught sight of Dee's arms around Jake in the foyer?

She refused to think about it. She'd done what she had to tonight. She'd held her tongue, buried her pride and let Dee turn the heat up under Jake. Hopefully it was enough to have him rethinking his marriage demand. She couldn't live in a relationship like this. Not without homicide being an option.

Lily pushed off the door, crossed her room and then pulled back the painting over her wall safe. She worked the combination with ease and slid out her jewelry case.

She had no intention of keeping the beautiful necklace from Jake, but she thought something so lovely should be treasured and protected until she could return it. She set the box on top of her vanity, right next to the colorful bouquet of lilies.

Being near him was the worst kind of emotional torture. Such a dichotomy of what she craved and what she loathed. She flipped open the lid of the box, noticing how the jewels glittered in the light.

A thought skittered across her mind. She could sell everything in the box and probably have enough money to be rid of Jake, to finish school and stay in an apartment until she could secure a teaching position. She could, except how much were her mother's pearls worth? She fingered the strand, wondering if anyone would care that the pink pearls were one of the few things she could remember her mother wearing. Eventually she could buy herself another diamond tennis bracelet, but it wouldn't be the one her father had gotten her for her high-school graduation.

She pursed her lips and blinked away the hot tears as she reached behind her and undid the clasp of Jake's necklace. She dropped it in the box, refusing to look at it as she removed her diamond teardrop earrings. College graduation from Dad.

It was stupid jewelry. Just things. She slammed the lid closed and shoved the box back in the safe, closing it quickly. They might be things, but they were tangible pieces of her memories. What was it Jake said? Memories live in your heart? What if it was broken? Might all the memories spill out with your tears?

Lily choked on a sob as she walked into her closet and shed her dress, leaving it in a pile on the floor. She didn't want it anymore, didn't want anything to remind her of how she'd felt while sitting at a table with Jake and his lover. She slipped on a nightgown and turned off the light. She stood at the window, staring at the dark night. Dee's car was gone, which gave her some modicum of relief. She wouldn't have to think about them together in the house. At least if he slept with Dee tonight, he had the decency to do it elsewhere.

She sunk down onto her bed and pressed her palms against her damp eyes, trying to stem the flow. Maybe she was as stupid as everyone thought. She was jealous of a woman she never wanted to be, wanted a man she could never actually have.

"Lily?" Jake's whisper drifted through the door and straightened her spine.

She listened and waited for him to try the handle, but he didn't. Instead, she heard his retreating footsteps. The darkness and silence must have been enough to convince him she'd fallen asleep. If only it would be so easy to convince him she still hated him.

Jake pulled on a pair of lounge pants and stalked out of his room. He'd been trying to fall asleep for hours. He'd even pulled one of Lily's Jane Austen books off the shelf, figuring he'd doze off for sure. No such luck. It just made him feel guilty.

He was indulging himself with watching Lily's jealousy

grow, and it hurt her. He had to stop, but he wasn't in a position to explain everything to her without losing what little advantage he had. Besides, if he started justifying his business relationships to her now, he'd be doing it for the rest of their lives.

He shook his head in disgust. With the way things were going, Lily might actually leave him alone and run away, no matter the consequences. She had him cornered, and his instinct was to fight. He could easily tempt her until her inhibitions melted, coerce her into accepting things the way he knew they should be. But what he really wanted was for her to realize all they could have if she'd only give herself freely.

He'd considered going to her tonight. He thought part of her issue with Dee might be insecurity. He'd been very clear that it was her he wanted, but she was inexperienced. While he admired her the more for not succumbing to the whims of the idiots she'd dated, Lily might see her innocence as a disadvantage. Besides, a physical release was what they both needed right now. But he didn't want her thinking he was using the necklace to barter for anything.

He made his way through the dark house without turning on any lights. The full moon provided just enough illumination to keep from bumping into things on his way to the kitchen. He pushed open the door and reached for the light switch, flicking it on.

Lily stood in front of the refrigerator, a carton of milk in her hand, at least until she spied him and dropped it with a gasp. His eyes widened at the sight of Lily in a pale pink nightie, her golden hair loose about her shoulders. The light material dipped low between her full breasts, delicately revealed the curve of her hips, and gave an alluring view of her bare thighs.

She wasn't so mesmerized. She cursed, then reached for a towel on the counter and bent low to clean up the spill. Jake pulled his libido back in check and moved to help her. He took the towel from her and she stood. He had to bite back a groan at how the hem of her nightie came right into his line of sight.

"I'm sorry," Lily said, walking around him and returning with another towel. "I didn't expect anyone."

"Obviously." He finished the task and stood, enjoying the way her chest hitched with each breath as he looked down at her. "What are you doing down here?"

"Having a glass of milk, or trying to anyway. That's what I do when I can't sleep." She kept her gaze locked on his, except for fleeting moments when it dropped to his bare chest.

He grinned, glad he wasn't the only one hyper-aware after midnight. "That's because you sleep alone."

Her cheeks pinked, but she recovered quickly, narrowing her eyes. "You know, I think you may be right. It's time I find someone willing to marry the penniless virgin and cure her insomnia."

She tried to walk past him, but he caught her arm, turned her around and pulled her flush against him. "Try it, and you'll find my patience exhausted quickly."

"While you expect me to live a life in perpetual

understanding of your need to go through mistresses faster than socks." She tried to shake off his hold, but he pulled her closer.

"I've never claimed to be a saint. But I'm not going to spend my life feeding into your insecurity. I want you, only you, and have from the moment I saw you.

"I watched you, this golden angel gliding across a room, and I wanted you to be looking for me, not one of those worthless idiots you dated. We hadn't even met, and I couldn't get you out of my mind. Maybe I did use your father to get closer to you. It seemed kismet that we were in the same industry. Will became my friend, but he became my partner because of you. I had no other choice. I had to protect you somehow, and you never would have looked twice at me had I not thrown myself in your way at every opportunity."

"You've been watching me?" Her haughty tone cut him to the quick. He was never going to be enough for her, never going to measure up to the vapid boys always trailing after her simply because he hadn't lived their life.

"And you've been watching me, wondering what it would be like if you were only brave enough to step outside your perfect world for a minute and indulge in all I can offer you." He took a step forward, moving them both until she was backed up against the kitchen table.

"What do you think you're doing?" Her eyes flashed with an emotion he hadn't seen in her yet. True fear, or excitement?

"What you've wanted me to do since you first started watching me. You think there's something beneath what the world sees. Maybe it's time I show you what that is."

Chapter Six

One hand threaded through her hair, massaging against her scalp until her eyelids started to droop.

"Emmaline is still in the house." Her voice broke with huskiness.

"Are you afraid you won't be able to stay quiet?" He brought his mouth down on hers, stealing her protests. He didn't force her, just moved slowly and softly, enjoying the gentle exploration. Lily escalated things, lifting her hands to his chest and pressing against his bare flesh. She parted her lips and deepened the kiss, answering his every stroke and raising him one better.

His hands caressed her shoulders, pushing the thin straps of her nightgown down and exposing her round breasts. She gasped as his hands cupped them, his thumbs brushing over the hardening tips. His lips slid along her jaw and nipped down the length of her neck, the strawberry scent of her shampoo and the silken feel of her hair against his cheek driving him on.

"We shouldn't do this," Lily whispered, but she didn't push him away. Her hands moved to his shoulders, around his back, setting fire to his skin everywhere she touched.

"It feels good, doesn't it?" His hands dropped to her waist and he hoisted her onto the table, sliding one of his thighs between hers before she realized what was happening and tried to squeeze them shut. "This will feel even better."

With the new alignment her bare breasts were at the perfect height for him to enjoy fully. His lips closed over one rosy peak and he sucked gently, tasting her with his tongue. She drew in a breath and arched her back, one hand twining in his hair. He kept on, learning the pressure and movements she liked best by the way her nails raked at his scalp and by how her thighs relaxed, allowing him to get even closer.

He pulled back and blew across the wet nipple, enjoying the way she shuddered before he turned his attention to her other breast. With one hand, he toyed with the sensitive bud, and the other he used to push up the short skirt of her nightie. He kneed the firm flesh of her outer thigh until he felt her spread her legs a little wider, giving him access to her most sensitive of places. His fingers found the rough lace of her panties and pushed them aside, parting the soft petals of her flesh.

She tensed around him, making him wonder if she'd ever allowed herself even this much pleasure from a man. He put the thought away quickly, knowing it didn't matter. He'd erase anyone who'd tried, teach her everything she needed to know.

As her hips arched into his hand an urgent need to

take her rushed through him. He'd never been so fiercely excited by a woman, so nearing the point where he lost control over his mind. Her hesitant touch only fueled him on, the ache in his groin begging him to sate them both.

But he wouldn't take her here, or like this. He wanted more than her passionate submission. He needed for her to want him in the same way, to come to him freely and forever. Being with her like this might change the game, but he knew better than to think it might end it.

The hand on her breast trailed to her shoulder, and then eased her back slowly. She gazed at him, her eyes shimmering and intoxicated with lust. Slender fingers reached out to him and he leaned down, feeling each fingertip against his scalp as his mouth covered hers, the budded tips of her breast pressing against his chest.

Her fingers stayed with him as he traced the kiss down her neck and between her breasts. He pushed up the silken hem of her nightie until it bunched about her waist. He trailed down the velvet skin of her stomach, dropping to one knee as he pressed slow kisses alongside her rounded hip.

She gave a shocked gasp as he parted the folds of her sex, making him smile at her ingrained resistance. He knew if he actually stopped she'd beg him not to. The air that entered her as a gasp escaped as low moan as his mouth touched the swollen lips of her sex.

His tongue lapped at her honeyed center, desire unfolding her like a blossoming flower. Deep within him, his own need flared. He held himself in check, pleasuring her until he found the apex of her passion and began to work the rigid nub.

Her fingernails ran over his scalp as her thighs began to quiver, breath racing through her body. As he fluttered his tongue against her clit he felt her desire swelling. She lifted her hips and twined her fingers in his hair.

"More, Jake," she said on a breath. "Please."

Pride coursed within him at having driven her past the point of abandon and he gave himself over to her pleasure. While his lips and tongue continued their wicked ministrations, he brought a hand to her core, sliding a finger against her wetness. She pressed against him and he eased inside her, able to feel every undulation, every shudder that throbbed through her as she melted against him in rapture, her passion cresting on a silent cry.

Jake rested his head on her soft thigh until he caught his breath, fighting to rein in his intense emotions. He rose, fixing the nightie he'd pushed aside in his rush to drive her mad with want. With a hand behind her back he pulled her up, holding her against his chest, his head resting on her silken hair.

He didn't want to let her go, but as she regained her senses her tiny hand trailed between them, dipping inside the waistband of his lounge pants. There was only so much he could restrain. He caught her wrist and took a step back, dropping her hand between them.

"Go to bed, Lily. You'll be able to sleep now."

"But—" Her eyes gleamed with a wonder that filled his

heart.

He shook his head. "Are you on the pill?"

She dropped her gaze, wrapping her arms around her waist.

"I didn't plan this, and I won't trap you." He swallowed hard, his mind making excuses, a laundry list of reasons why he could indulge himself right now.

"But we could..." She looked from his face down his body until her cheeks pinked in embarrassment.

"Angel, I doubt you even know how." He helped her down from the table, and with a hand on the small of her back ushered her toward the door. "Go to bed, Lily. Sweet dreams."

Lily had lost focus on the evolving definition of love in the works of Jane Austen. Not a great idea when she had two months to finish her thesis. Maybe the texture of irony would work better. Or the new wave of Jane Austen apocrypha. She scribbled furiously in her notebook, outlining a class featuring the books and movies based on Jane Austen's characters. A class she'd never teach if she didn't finish her thesis.

The entire weekend had been spent on her class work. She told herself she wanted to get ahead since she was working, but really she didn't want to fall asleep. Sleep brought dreams of Jake. She hadn't spoken to him since the night in the kitchen. Her cheeks heated just thinking about it. Not a word from him all weekend, and this morning at the office she learned he was off scouting projects throughout the country. Great to know what they'd done meant so much to him. And just like everything she tried to think about, it all circled back to Jake Tolliver.

She groaned in frustration, looking out the window of the cozy bistro she'd come to for lunch. When she was meeting her father for lunch she always suggested they come here. He usually ran late and the large tables gave her plenty of room to work while she waited.

She'd even come here with her friends since it was near the downtown campus of the university. But both her school friendships and those with people she'd known longer had evaporated. The newspapers had a lot to do with it. As much as she hated it, she understood how society worked. She'd been tarnished by the aftermath of bad investments and the tawdry escapades published about her father. It was too much of a risk for some of her former friends to acquaint with her now.

The people at school weren't as cold, but they'd never been exactly friendly. They didn't understand what had happened, the ramifications of someone else's mistakes. But Lily had never fit in with them anyway. She didn't have time for sorority pranks or fraternity parties, then or now. School was for learning, that hadn't changed.

The only difference was instead of filling her day with people, she filled it with either work or school. The only people who actually asked how she was doing were Emmaline and Jake. Well, Jake when he could be bothered to pretend he cared about her as more than a trophy.

No more thinking about Jake. He was gone, and she had better things to think about. Like focusing on her thesis. She turned back to her notebook, but her gaze snagged on the slim man walking through the door. Her first instinct was to smile as she recognized Ian Landon. They'd dated for a while before he'd transferred to a different accounting firm in Florida. But since he'd been away she didn't know if he'd heard the news about her father. She didn't want to be snubbed, and she didn't want to have to explain, so instead of making eye contact she opened up the copy of *Pride and Prejudice*.

"Lily, how have you been?" A warm voice wrapped around her.

She looked up and smiled. "Hello, Ian."

"Are you waiting for someone or can I join you?" He pulled out the chair opposite her and sat, not waiting for a response. "I heard about your father. I am sorry." He reached for her hand and she let him take it, needing him to be sincere. She needed for someone to remember she was a person underneath the veneer, not a student more number than name, or a doll learning about an architecture firm by rote.

She nodded her thanks. "What are you doing in town?"

"I'm on an assignment here. I'll be in the city for six weeks. And what have you been up to?"

"I'm taking classes at the university."

"Are you still playing at that? I thought you would have given it up by now."

She clenched her teeth against explaining that she was getting a graduate degree. She didn't need to argue with him. "I'm also working at the firm my father owned."

"You have a job?" He grimaced in mock disgust. "How awful for you."

"Actually, it's quite nice. I'm learning about the business, about why my father cared so much about it." She meant every word. She might not like having to avoid Jake's scrutiny, but she did enjoy learning what the company was all about.

Ian stared at her blankly, reminding Lily of how so many of the people in that social set looked at her. They'd all thought she wasted her energy trying to earn a degree, energy better spent in day spas and shopping malls.

"What have you been up to, Ian? Tell me about Florida. I can see you enjoy the sun."

He raked a hand through his sun-streaked hair and rubbed on his tanned chin. He told her about beaches and clubs, about clients and golf courses, until she had to tense her jaw to keep from yawning. Her mind was wandering and she had the distinct impression she was being watched. Wary of the reporters she'd so far eluded, she looked around.

Her heart stalled as she spied Jake's dark gaze on her. Seated across from him was Dee Gibson who smiled at her while shaking her head slightly. Lily turned her attention back to Ian, but didn't hear a word.

How long had they been in the restaurant? When she'd come in she'd been so focused on eating and reading she hadn't noticed anyone else. Had they been watching her as she sat alone?

"Who are you looking at?" Ian turned, but Lily couldn't watch. "Tolliver. Does he still follow you with his eyes everywhere he goes? It was damned unnerving."

"Why?" she asked, taking a drink from her ice water.

"He was always so blatant about it, looking after you as if I meant to run off with you. Your father must have put him up to it."

He had no idea. "I should be getting back to work."

"Of course. You know, I'd like to see you again while I'm in town. Give us a chance to catch up properly."

"That's sweet of you, but between school and work I'm really busy."

Ian grinned. "Same Lily, always politely keeping people from getting too close. Let me take you out some time, just as a break from the toil your life has become."

She would have said no, wanted to, but she felt Jake's stare heavily on her. He had no right, especially as he sat there with his lover. Lily smiled at Ian, not for Ian but to show Jake he couldn't intimidate her.

"You're right. It might be nice to have someone to meet for lunch."

Ian walked her out and to the stop where she picked up the streetcar that would take her back to the office. He pulled her close as the car pulled up, pressing a kiss to her lips. "I'll call you to set something up. Tomorrow even."

Too shocked to say anything, Lily stepped up onto the car, using the blocks to get her bearings again. She'd gone out with Ian for months, but she'd only kissed him a few times. Did he think they'd be picking up where they'd left off?

She didn't want to lead Ian on. Maybe lunch wasn't such a good idea after all. When the streetcar arrived at the building, she got off but didn't make it but a few steps when someone grabbed her arm and turned her around.

Jake tried to tamp down the rage coursing through him, threatening the rigid control he cultivated. He wasn't sure he was capable of sanity right now. He'd been annoyed when he saw Lily with the twit she used to date, but watching her kiss another man had his blood boiling. Maybe Dee was right and Lily was playing him for a fool.

He'd followed her out of the restaurant to find out what was really going on, just in time to see them together. He'd hopped in his car and sped to the office, pulling to the curb as she got off the streetcar. In seconds he was beside her, taking her by the arm and leading her to his car.

"Jake? What are you doing?"

He stopped short, glaring down at her. "Do you want to have this conversation in public? I've been trying to keep you out of the papers."

"You've been trying a lot of things," she said in a harsh whisper. "You have no right to be angry with me."

He clenched his jaw, wanting so badly to shake some

sense into her it scared him. He released his hold and stepped to the car, holding open the back door.

"I have to get back to work." She pressed her lips into a thin line.

"If you want a job, you get in the car."

She stared up at him with wide eyes, but didn't object. Once she slid into the seat he got in beside her and slammed the door to release some of his frustration. It didn't work.

"What the hell did you think you were doing?"

She moved to the far door, pulling her body away from him. "Me? I was having lunch. If you thought it was more, maybe it was your own guilt echoing back at you."

"What do I have to be guilty for?" Fury almost choked him. After all he'd done for her, years of devotion, she expected him to be some pathetic cuckolded pushover. "I wasn't the one kissing people in the street."

She opened her mouth to say something, but her expression changed from open to angry before she spoke. "A little afternoon delight with your mistress is so much more acceptable?"

"We're not talking about me."

"Of course not. Because what you do isn't open for negotiation. It's me who needs to mold myself into the perfect wife for you. Well, you can take that notion and—"

"I am not trying to mold you into anything." He ran a hand through his hair, hating that he'd ever let her believe there was something going on between him and

Dee. She probably wouldn't have believed his denial then, and she definitely wouldn't now. "I don't want you to change, Lily. But kissing idiots on the sidewalk isn't like you."

"How would you know? Oh that's right. You've been watching me. Studying exactly how to get me to do what you want."

"I don't want you to do anything you don't want to."

"Except marry you and turn the other cheek while you entertain yourself with a collection of other women."

"I've told you before, jealousy doesn't suit you."

"And it looks so good on you."

"I will not be played for a fool. I've given you so much. I'm allowing you to play this game with the firm, letting you stay in the home you love, and not pressuring you in any way. But other men are not allowed. I will not compete for you."

She raised an eyebrow. "Scared you won't measure up?"

"You're just trying to distract yourself. If you think that tool will measure up to me, you'll be sorely disappointed. You want me, and you wish you didn't. Let's not drag other people into this. Or I'll have to make some calls and ship him back beneath the rock he crawled out from."

She lifted her chin. "Ian doesn't work for you."

"How do you think he got his promotion? Lots of people owe me favors, Lily. You know, they have offices in

Alaska. Above the Arctic Circle. Is that where you want to go?"

"It would be warmer than being with you."

A low and sinister laugh escaped him. "You can't see other people. You will marry me, sooner rather than later, and because you want to. If you try and play me, you'll regret it." He reached out, running his fingers down her smooth cheek. "I'll never hurt you, but whomever dares touch you will answer to me.

"You are mine, Lily. I will wait for you to want me, but I will not let someone else have you."

He didn't stop to analyze the primitive claim, didn't care that he was acting more animal than man. She'd reduced him to it, which was why he had to get away from her before he did what he swore he wouldn't and used their mutual attraction to make her give in.

Lily looked up at him, but without the fear or intimidation he'd grown accustomed to. Challenge, pure and simple, and it was the sexiest thing he'd ever seen. He lowered his head and kissed her, claiming erotic rights in a way so primal it would throw men back generations if he were ever to state them out loud.

He savored the taste of her, relished the texture, delighted in the soft strawberry scent he'd forever recognize as hers. She opened for him without protest, returning his kiss with a fervor she never had before. He kissed her until her fingers gripped the front of his shirt, until she moaned and leaned into him.

Jake broke the kiss, leaning his forehead against hers

as they both caught their breath, taken aback by how quickly the fire between them could blaze out of control. He felt like a teenager, cornering her in kitchens and the back seat of cars. But if they ever found themselves in the vicinity of a bed he knew he couldn't be trusted anymore, and she wouldn't hold him back.

And that was why he'd decided to go on a tour of all the active projects in the country. Yes, it needed to be done, but he could delegate it. Only he didn't trust himself to be near Lily.

"I'm going to be gone for a month. Do I need to take you with me so I can keep an eye on you?"

She pulled away from him, smoothing a hand over her hair. "I don't need you watching me. I'll be busy with school and work, and we have a deal. By the time you get back I'll know even more about the firm."

Jake shook his head and turned, opened the door and climbed out. He reached into the car and pulled Lily to her feet. "Stay focused on yourself, Angel. This game you're playing is one we can both win if you play by the rules. Cross me and you won't be the only one who regrets it."

He released her, not minding one bit that her confident façade faltered at his threat. He meant every word.

In the weeks since Jake had left her shaky kneed on the sidewalk, Lily had only heard from him via email.

Which was an amazing relief. It gave her time to school her physical responses and allowed her to focus on finishing her thesis.

She'd been crazy to think about changing it this late in the game. All the research was done, the paper outlined and drafted. So what if she was having personal issues with defining love on a sliding scale? What mattered was making her deadline and keeping a clear head during her review with the examination committee.

She hit send, propelling her work to her advisor. The last step before she revised the final draft and had to face the review committee. Everything was lining up, and she'd never been more exhausted in her life. Between classes, the thesis and work, she was only managing a few hours of sleep at night.

It was a wonder she even knew what department to report to. Jake had her in a different unit every week. Even though he hadn't been around, he'd checked in with whoever was training her each week and passed on where she'd go next. She'd learned a lot, but it meant she constantly felt off-balance, never getting her footing in any one area.

When she'd arrived at work today she'd learned Jake was back. She'd been able to know where he was easily enough. His picture had been taken escorting a Hollywood starlet to the launch party for her new restaurant, made the business section in Chicago when he sold the apparel company he'd told her he'd bought, and showed up at a fashion show with Dee Gibson in New York. Not that she'd been Googling him. Much.

When she got his email summoning her from her desk in accounting, she'd thought about ignoring it. It was Monday, and she usually met Ian for lunch. She'd been clear with him that she had too much going on to get involved, but he met her anyway. It made her feel normal to talk with someone from her old life. But knowing Jake's opinion of her doing anything with Ian, she half thought he'd sent for her so she'd miss the date.

With a sigh of resignation, she signed off her computer and made her way upstairs. There was no one in the reception area of Jake's office so she knocked on the ajar door to his office and pushed it open.

He sat in command of the glass-and-steel room, the phone tucked between his neck and shoulder as his fingers strummed over the keyboard to his computer. He didn't look up, only acknowledging her with a brusque wave of his hand and pointing at the black leather chair opposite his desk.

She sat, not knowing what else to do. From the conversation she garnered he was dealing with the project manager of a construction site, which she'd learned from her week in the projects department could take a while. The construction team liked to be listened to.

Glancing around the office, she looked for some sign of life. Everything was cool and clean, not a picture or stray scrap of paper in sight. She wondered if he'd personalized his office upstairs at Tolliver Enterprises more than he had this one at Tolliver-Harris. Or maybe there was nothing personal about the man.

He set down the phone but returned to his computer, typing furiously. She noted how his profile spoke of power and authority, how the set of his chin gave away his stubborn streak. His lips were firm and sensual, even when pursed in concentration. Lily thought she might need to remind him she was in the room when he spoke.

"You'll need to bring your things up here. You'll be my PA for the rest of your time with the company. However long you want that to be."

Lily blinked, unsure if he was talking to her. "But I don't know anything about being a personal assistant."

Finally, he turned his body to face hers. "You didn't know anything about public relations either, and they said you were great. I'm not claiming I'd want you running the payroll department or consulting on design, but you do know the company well enough to coordinate my day. Besides, I need to keep an eye on you."

"I don't need babysitting. I think I'm proving I can be useful here, that I can understand the business my father built." She gave a thin smile, doubting he'd ever let her out of their deal so easily, but hopeful all the same.

"You asked to learn about the firm, not just parts of it. As my assistant you'll see how all the different units work together. Besides, Helen went out on maternity leave while I was gone. My PAs upstairs have been picking up the slack, but it's not good for the autonomy of the firm to have them handle everything."

"But I can't work every day. I have classes."

"And as much as I'd like to spend all my time

designing, I have other businesses to run. Besides, you have half of this week off for Thanksgiving, then three weeks left of classes, and then we're only two weeks until the wedding."

Their gazes locked at the mention of the wedding that was never to be. He arched a dark brow as if daring her to disagree, but then continued before she had a chance to formulate a response.

"Helen will be back in January. She actually planned when she was going to have the baby so she'd get the holidays off." He turned back to his computer, using the mouse to click his way through something.

Lily might have been flattered that he had bothered to learn her school schedule, but she was too busy trying to think of another reason she couldn't work so closely with him. It was all so ridiculous, if he'd just drop this outlandish marriage scheme she'd actually be grateful for all he'd done for her. As her mind whirled through excuses, she realized the job might be the best option. She'd learned a lot while working, but nothing easily transferable into a position with another company. However, working as a PA rather than a continual trainee would likely mean she'd have an easier time finding her next job.

The phone rang on Jake's desk. He placed his hand on it, and then looked up at her. "You can put your things in the desk outside. I think Helen has a to-do list out there you can use to get started. And there is always the team upstairs if you have any questions."

Before she could ask any of him, Jake picked up the phone and started talking. It gave Lily hope that he was planning on ignoring her, just as he had done the last few weeks. As she collected her things, she started to wonder if his whole marriage idea wasn't waning. Her stomach tightened at the thought of being free of him, but she wouldn't let herself think too hard on why.

She'd just slid her purse into an empty drawer and started reading over the detailed to-do list on the desk when she heard Jake bellow for her from his office. She gritted her teeth at his tone, but grabbed a tablet and pen before marching back to him. She'd do this job as she had all the others, even if it meant being at Jake Tolliver's beck and call.

"We need to head out to the old school site. There are some problems that have to be taken care of today."

Lily recalled the project. Tolliver-Harris was reconfiguring an old Catholic boarding school, redesigning it into a destination hotel with a pub, bakery, and with the former gym serving as a movie theater. The firm had done similar projects for the company in the past, jobs she knew her father had worked on.

"Go on, get your coat. We're leaving." Jake crossed his office until he was almost next to her, and opened the closet by the door.

"I'm going? But it's snowing." And she was wearing open-toed heels. Not the smartest thing to wear in winter, but they matched her dress and how was she to guess she'd see anything more chilling than the parking garage today?

"Yes, princess, it is. Don't worry, you can't freeze if you keep moving. Bring something to take notes on. Actually, check the desk outside for the PDA Helen used. It should have access to some of the files we might need."

Lily dashed out of the office, dialing the phone as she searched the drawers. She found the PDA just as Ian answered. She explained that she had to cancel lunch as quickly as she could.

"Don't tell me you have a better offer." His tone was cold and disapproving.

"I have to work. I'm starting a new position and I can't get away today."

"That's silly. It's your father's company."

It had been, but it wasn't anymore. "It's important to me that I do a good job."

"But it's not like what you do there is important. Aren't you just answering the phone? Surely someone else can do that while you're at lunch."

Lily sat up straighter. He hadn't heard a word she'd said about her job in the last month. "I'm a personal assistant for the head of the company. And I'll be too busy at one of our project sites to have lunch."

"Tolliver has you working as his secretary? Oh come on, Lily. You have to be smarter than that."

Lily blinked, unable to believe he'd just implied she was stupid. Granted their lunches were mostly talking about him and his telling her what all her old acquaintances were up to, but she'd told him about her job, her work on her thesis. Yet he was treating her like some bubble-headed twit. She just didn't have the time in her life for that, not anymore. Working had shown her she was more than society parties and academia. She could take care of herself and didn't need anyone in her life who didn't agree.

"Ian, I don't think I'll be able to have lunch with you again."

"Come now. I didn't mean to upset you. But you obviously aren't thinking about Tolliver's angle. If he wants *you* as a personal assistant, the emphasis is on the personal." She didn't fail to catch the sarcasm thick in his tone. "You don't know anything about running someone's office."

Anger percolated inside of her. She'd wasted four Monday lunches with this man. She should have stuck to her books. "Don't worry about me. I hope your project goes well. Have a safe trip back to Florida."

She rang off, only just managing not to slam the phone down. When she turned to grab her coat, she caught Jake glowering at her from his office doorway. He stared for a minute but didn't say a word as he started to walk toward the elevator.

Lily grabbed her things and tried to keep up with him.

Chapter Seven

Jake kept two steps ahead of Lily, not wanting to risk saying something to her she'd throw in his face later. He tried to keep his mind on the issues with the old school project, but he kept thinking about Lily and her trust-fund boyfriend. Seeing her with someone else made him crazy, made him feel like his father. And that was the most unpleasant feeling in the world.

Jake kept walking, forcing himself to focus on the problems he could fix. The project manager claimed the designs for the refurbishing of the former boarding school into a hotel had major flaws. He'd hoped the man had been overreacting, but standing outside the former dormitory that was about to see new life as guest suites, he knew the plans Will Harris had drawn hadn't been his best. Which meant Jake would be redoing them. Personally. As soon as possible.

The McTarnahan brothers were one of the best clients the firm had. They reconstructed historic structures into hotels and restaurants throughout the West Coast, and Jake wasn't willing to lose the account. He'd told Lily this morning that he didn't spend every day designing, but now he just might have to.

He stopped and turned, motioning for Lily to catch up. He winced at how cold she looked, her high heels wet with slush and mud. She'd have to learn to be more prepared for the things that came up in a business like this. He wanted her to learn what it was her father had done, what he loved to do, so that she'd understand them both better. He couldn't let her stubbornness or impractical footwear get in the way of that.

"Do you know how to work the PDA?" he asked as she came to stand beside him.

She rolled her eyes. "It's three versions back from mine. You really should upgrade."

"Fine. Order a new one when we get back to the office. But right now I need you to take some notes so I can get started on the fixes." He kept walking, telling her what needed fixing immediately. When they were spied by the project manager and construction foreman, Jake walked toward them quickly, introducing Lily and promising what he needed to.

Lily wandered between the buildings while he listened to the concerns of the men. He couldn't help but keep an eye on her, wishing she would stay still so he wouldn't feel so distracted. He'd thought keeping her close would help him concentrate, but really it was not knowing what she wanted that kept him on edge.

His entire world tilted as he watched her disappear. One moment she'd been walking beside the gymnasium building and the next she'd vanished beside it. He gave a shout and ran toward where she'd been, his heart hammering between his ears.

Lily lay wide-eyed at the bottom of a trench, PVC pipes along one side of her. Mud and slush splattered all over her coat and bare legs, leeching into her hair. Jake cursed and hopped carefully into the furrow, not sure if he should move her.

"That was embarrassing." Lily closed her eyes and pulled her legs up. Jake breathed a sigh of relief that she could move them.

"Do you hurt anywhere?" He surveyed her from the closer angle, not seeing anything out of place.

"Does my pride count?" She shivered and moved to get up. Jake put a hand behind her back and eased her to sitting.

"Are you sure nothing hurts?"

"My head and my bum, but I'm more cold and mortified than anything."

The men he'd been speaking with appeared at the side of the ditch, looking down at them. Jake explained that they were fine and allowed one of the men to help him out. He then reached down and lifted Lily free. She squealed when he tried to set her down.

"My shoes came off."

Jake looked down at her bare feet and the icy ground, then up at her flushed cheeks. If he hadn't been so terrified she'd hurt herself, he might have laughed. Instead he lifted her into his arms and carried her toward the car.

He set her inside and covered her with his coat, tensing at how she was shivering. He rounded the car and quickly had the heat on high as he sped away from the site. He hated that he'd brought her there unprepared, that he hadn't warned her to be more careful, that his heart still raced with fear.

"Where are we going?" she asked between chattering teeth.

"The emergency room to get you checked out."

"Please don't. I'm fine, I swear. It's bad enough I had an audience, I don't want to tell even more people what a klutz I am."

"You hit your head." Fear and concern knotted inside his gut.

"I've done worse with a kitchen cupboard. Really, I'm fine. I just need to get changed and warmed up. I'll be back at work this afternoon."

"No, you won't. And you're freezing. You couldn't possibly make it all the way back to the house without developing hypothermia. We're going to the ER."

"Jake, that's a bit extreme." She fought him with words, though her body shook convulsively. He'd been wet and muddy when they'd started the car, but now he was starting to sweat from the intensity of the heater. She was obviously more than just a little chilled.

"I'm not taking any chances with you."

"If you take me to a hospital I will walk out." Her voice trembled with cold. "And if you try and strong-arm me, they'll probably have you investigated for battery."

Jake cut his gaze to her at the stoplight. "Are you threatening me while I am trying to keep you healthy?"

"You threaten me all the time. It's not just architecture I've learned about." She wrapped her arms around her body, but the shaking didn't stop.

He gunned it when the light turned green, taking his frustration out on the car. Goodness knows what she'd come up with next. He pulled into the garage at his apartment and coasted into his parking space.

"Where are we?" Lily asked as he helped her out of the car.

"The penthouse. Should I carry you, or can you walk? I wouldn't want you to accuse me of kidnapping you."

She rolled her eyes. "If you'll take me back to the office I can take my car and go home."

He shook his head. "It's a half-hour drive, at least. If you don't want to go to the hospital then you're coming upstairs and getting warmed up."

She opened her mouth, probably to fight with him some more, but the chills must have gotten the best of her because she didn't say a word as he led her to the elevator. The mirrored ride to the top showed him just how ridiculous they both looked smeared with mud and dripping with water. What a mess they'd gotten into.

Once inside his apartment, he led her to the guest bathroom and started the shower, testing the temperature of the water with his hand. When he was satisfied it was warm enough, he pulled open a drawer the housekeeper kept stocked with toiletries.

"Stay in the shower until you've warmed up. It makes me feel like an ass when I argue with a woman whose teeth are chattering."

She lifted her chin and looked up at him. "Stop snapping at me all the time and you won't feel like such an ass. You're not the only one whose opinion matters."

"Of course not." Jake blinked. If he didn't think her opinion mattered they'd have been married a month ago. He looked her up and down, his gaze stalling on her shivering, pink hands. "Do you need help getting out of your clothes?"

"You wish. I'll be fine."

He merely nodded and watched her struggle with the buttons of her coat. He stepped back to her and undid them quickly before she could protest. He reached around and unzipped her dress, but didn't trust himself to do more. Instead he turned to go before the steam in the room went to his head.

Lily perched on the seat in the shower, hot water pelting down on her. Her head was pounding and a bruise was developing on her leg before her eyes. Propping her elbows on her knees, she let her head drop into her hands. It had taken the last of her energy just to wash her hair. The idea of getting out of the shower was absolutely laughable.

She'd been so lucky not to really hurt herself in the fall. She was exhausted and hadn't paid attention the way she should have. What little energy she had seemed focused on what Jake was thinking or doing instead of keeping herself safe. If she didn't keep her guard up she'd wind up giving in. Or she'd wind up beneath him.

A vision of exactly that flashed in her mind and she sat straight up. She couldn't go there. Not even in her fantasies. It was one area he had her beaten and she didn't want to think about it at all.

Lily shut off the shower, hoping it was just the water making her hot. She toweled off and then a cold chill of panic raced down her back. Her clothes were soggy and muddy on the bathroom floor. Even if she had the energy to rinse off the dirt in the sink there was no way she could put them back on.

With a groan, she wrapped the towel around her body as tightly as she could manage. She didn't want any wardrobe malfunctions. She opened the bathroom door and peeked out, seeing nothing but the polished floor of the long hallway. Too focused on staying warm when she'd come in, she wasn't sure which way anything might be.

"Jake?" she called out, holding the towel to her body.

He burst out of a doorway, slowing when he caught sight of her. She couldn't take her eyes off him, his hair wet and tousled, the muscles of his chest defined and tan, a pair of worn jeans, and bare feet. Even in her fantasies he'd never looked this good.

"Are you all right?" He came toward her. The proximity of his overpowering maleness made her want to tighten her hold on the towel, but that would have meant crushing her own ribs.

"Fine. It's just that I don't have any clothes."

"You don't need them."

Her eyes widened. Part of her wanted to run, but another more sinister part felt like dropping the towel. Luckily she'd never let that part have a say in what she did and now was not the time to start.

"I need something to wear back to the office so I can get my car. A T-shirt or sweats or something."

He shook his head. "You're going to bed."

"Not with you!"

"Lily, you've had quite the morning. You're not going back to work."

"Fine, but I'm not staying here." Her mind floundered for a way out, a solution that made sense. Unfortunately, it seemed the fall had knocked the sense clean out of her.

"I don't see how you have much choice."

His hand snaked out and melted into her shoulder. Somehow he melded into her so much she found herself entering a bedroom. The sight of the large bed with the covers pulled back stiffened her spine and had her heart racing.

"Relax, Angel. This is the guest room. You're safe from the big bad wolf. But you do need to get out of that towel. It's wet and you'll get cold again."

She shook her head. "No way."

"What if I promise to turn around?" His voice softened, losing the steely edge.

"I'm not going to get naked with you."

"You liked it last time." With a flick of his wrist her towel dropped and she went scrambling for the bed. He delivered a quick swat to her bottom before she was able to sit down and wrap the sheets around her. "You can't keep me here." Blood pounded in her ears, her headache intensifying.

He shrugged. "If I planned on keeping you here, I wouldn't have bought an estate outside of town for you. What I want now is for you to rest."

"You can't dictate how things are going to be and expect me to respond like a puppet. The second you leave I'll find something to put on and get a cab downstairs. Hell, I'd even wear something of Dee's."

He shot a commanding look at her. "I'm not going to let you kill yourself. I wish you'd forget this damn bargain and just marry me. This is getting out of hand."

"I am not marrying you. You know that."

"I know nothing of the sort. You don't want to marry me right now, but you will eventually."

"I don't want the life you're offering."

"You can't think Ian can give you more. That boy can't afford you."

She suddenly felt colder than she had lying in the slush. "You might be used to women who place a dollar value on their pride, but I am not one of them. You cannot talk to me like I am some kind of..." The words didn't come as her face crumpled, her strength failing her as she choked on a sob. She just didn't have it in her to fight with him, not while she was trapped here and her head felt as if it were splitting in two.

He cursed and sat next to her on the bed. She didn't want him to touch her, didn't want him anywhere near her, but she couldn't find the strength to push him away. She might have discovered it somewhere if he'd done more than wrap her in his arms and hold her close.

Tears dripped down her cheeks, her throat growing tight and heavy. Each time she sobbed her head hurt worse, so she recovered as fast as she could manage. She pulled away from him, wiping her face with the sheet and laying her head down on the soft pillow. Feeing his heavy stare on her, she pulled the sheet over her head and wished both him and the headache away.

"I'm sorry I made you go to the site today."

His apology startled her so much she peeked out from beneath the sheet. "You're just sorry I fell. Worried about getting sued?"

He grinned down at her, his mouth curved with tenderness as he reached his hand out to caress her cheek. "You scared me. I thought maybe you really had hurt yourself when you started crying. You're stronger than that."

"I have a headache and I'm being held against my will. I think I've earned a tantrum or two."

He lay down next to her on the bed, making her eyes widen in shock. But he didn't do anything but stare at her for what seemed like an eternity. She searched the dark depths of his gaze for answers, but she'd forgotten the questions.

"You might have a concussion. Do you hurt anywhere else?"

One of his hands drifted into her damp hair, massaging her neck and then her scalp. She closed her eyes and enjoyed the sensation until he found a sensitive spot that made her wince.

"I wish you'd have gone to the ER."

"Me too. I doubt they'd have trapped me naked in a bed."

His laugh warmed her, the tension swirling out of her body as his warm hands brushed over her shoulders and arms. He found a sore spot on an elbow that was sure to be a bruise. If she weren't so exhausted she might worry about how black and blue she'd be tomorrow.

"Lily, put this on."

She blinked to awareness, her heart hammering as she looked about the strange room. Jake's guest room. She must have drifted off after her shower. She reached a hand to her head. It was still aching, but her hair was nearly dry. The doorbell chimed and Jake dropped a folded T-shirt on the bed beside her.

"Put on the shirt, Angel." Jake turned and left the room.

Lily's head spun as she sat up and tried to get her bearings. The fall, the shower, the slap on her rump all came back to her. In a flash she grabbed the shirt and wriggled into it, thankful to finally have something on. Not that she could catch a cab in an oversized t-shirt, but it was better than stark naked.

The voices in the hallway had her sitting up, trying to listen and figure out just what was going on. Jake entered the room first. She realized he'd gotten dressed, a soft black sweater and worn jeans hugging his body. Behind him came a beautiful woman with long raven hair and a friendly smile. Her grassy green sweater set off her green eyes perfectly, but it all served to confuse Lily further.

Jake sat next to her on the bed, taking her hand. With everything such a jumble in her mind she didn't want to pull away.

"Angel, this is Susanna Kaye. She's a doctor."

She ran a hand through her hair, not sure what to think. "I didn't think doctors made house calls anymore."

"I don't for anyone but friends." Susanna stepped forward and held out her hand. "It's nice to finally meet you, Lily. Though I wish it were under better circumstances."

Susanna sat on the bed, opening a large bag she'd carried in with her.

"Wait a minute," Lily said. "Did something else happen?" Maybe she'd had a seizure and that was why she was feeling so out of it.

"You do remember that you fell?" He stared at her until she nodded. "With a concussion it's better to be safe than sorry." Jake squeezed her hand and then rose from the bed. "I think her head and shoulder took the brunt of it, but she has bruises on her elbow and legs too. I'll be outside if you need me."

"What's going on?" Lily asked as Susanna laid some instruments beside her on the bed.

"You scared him," Susanna smiled and clicked a small device that shone a light in Lily's eye. She reared her head back, but then relaxed as the light moved to the other eye. "I've never heard him in such a panic. In fact, I thought he was quite incapable of overreacting. Have you had any dizziness?"

"Dizziness? When I first sat up, but I think I just moved to fast." Jake was panicked? Maybe he thought she was serious about suing him.

"When was the last time you ate?" Susanna's small fingers probed along Lily's neck to her collar bones.

"Breakfast."

"That's more likely to be it. Are you normally tired in the afternoon?"

Lily shook her head and watched as the doctor examined one arm and shoulder and then the other. "But I haven't been sleeping very much. I've been working and keeping up with school."

Susanna merely nodded, putting on her stethoscope. "I love Jane Austen. I don't see anything more than a story though. I think we're hardwired for what we're supposed to do." She pressed the chest piece against Lily's ribs. "I've always wanted to know how the body works. I never seem to get tired of it. You're probably the same way with books."

She was actually, but what surprised her was how much this woman seemed to know about her. Jake couldn't have related much between the entry and her room.

"Can you take a deep breath and hold it for a few seconds?"

Lily did, glad for the moment to collect her thoughts. "How long have you known Jake?"

"Forever. We grew up in the same housing project. He was the one who helped me fill out the scholarship forms to get into the university. He's always helping someone, but you already knew that."

That made her his latest pet project. She looked at Susanna, wondering if she'd been one of his improvement schemes too. Maybe he reconstructed women the way he did buildings, and then walked away to find someone else to captivate his attention for a while. How could she make him understand that no matter how much he built up her exterior, she didn't have the internal structure to withstand the blow of being cast aside for another?

"I think you're fine." Susanna packed her things back in her satchel. "A mild concussion and some bruises. Nothing a good meal and rest won't take care of. Ibuprofen can help with the achiness you'll feel next time you wake up. Any questions?"

Besides just what was Susanna's relationship with Jake? "Not really. Thank you for coming over. It was very kind of you."

"I'd do anything for Jake." Susanna stood and lifted her bag. "You're very lucky."

Lily watched her leave the room, knowing the woman wasn't referring to the fall. She sank back into the pillows and wondered just how many women were walking around in love with Jake Tolliver.

"What exactly did you tell Susanna about me?" Lily sipped at her tea, trying not to seem too interested.

"That you fell at the site and every time I tried to wake you up, you kept telling me to let you sleep, which isn't good if you had a concussion. Why?" Jake leaned in the doorway of the bedroom holding a tray with the remnants of their lunch.

"She knew what I'm studying."

He shrugged and left the room without a word. Lily finished her tea and set the mug on the nightstand. The painkillers had worked their magic, as had the food. She might be able to rest if her mind ever slowed down.

Now it was busy making a list of all she had to do before classes tomorrow as well as coming up with myriad explanations for how the good doctor knew so much about her. Since she studied story and motivation for sport, she had a million ways the plot could twist, and none of them in her favor.

"I'm going to work in the den." Jake leaned against the doorjamb again and ran his fingers through his hair, leaving it mussed for the first time she'd ever seen. "You should sleep. If you need anything I'll be right here."

"I need to go home, Jake. Besides, I don't want to stay here and cramp your style. What if one of your girlfriends was to find me here? I'm not in any shape for a cat fight."

"I think you hit your head harder than you think." He crossed the room and sat down next to her on the bed. "Just because you want to be with me doesn't mean every woman in the free world does. Half of them maybe, but not all."

Lily closed her gaping mouth. "I'm not going to be with you. I've made that very clear. I don't understand why you don't find someone more suitable for your breeding plan."

"Breeding plan?" Jake laughed and leaned back against the padded headboard. "No one is more suitable for either of us." He let out a long sigh and turned to look at her. "Nothing has ever come easy for me. I've had to fight for everything I have. If I gave up on everything that didn't fall in my lap I'd have been a junior partner at the firm and we would have lost the house. And you still wouldn't have looked twice at me."

Lily turned toward him, anxiety trilling through her veins. She didn't trust herself this close to him, an intimate distance that belied their relationship. But for once they were talking without yelling, so maybe he'd hear her this time.

"Marrying me is just part of a game to you, something you don't want to lose out of pride. You see me as some token of success that will validate all you've attained. But once you've had your fill of me you'll toss me aside like all the others. There are women that can handle that, some that would welcome it for the alimony payments alone, but not me. I do appreciate everything you've done to protect me, and I'll even admit a month ago I needed it. But we have to stop this."

"I agree."

At his words Lily breathed a sigh of relief and closed her eyes, thankful he'd finally heard her. She glimpsed at freedom until she felt his mouth touch hers. He tasted of rich coffee and persuasion. Flames of desire licked through her and she kissed him back, not consciously, but because she couldn't not. The mingling of lips and tongues felt as natural and comforting as breathing, as soft and gentle as his fingertips against her scalp, tilting her head back for more.

Jake eased his lips from hers and framed her face in his large hands. "I'll never have enough of you, Lily. This kind of chemistry doesn't happen often, if at all. I will go to my grave still wanting you, and as much as I want to run from it, to keep us both safe from being consumed by it, I've never taken the safe route."

When he looked at her like this, as if there was more behind his words than lust and ambition, she almost believed him. His hands slid from her face, skimming her body, and she wanted there to be more. She wanted to buy the snake oil he was selling, wanted to believe. The more time she spent with him the less she thought about their stupid bargain, about his ridiculous proposal, about anything but the way he could make her feel with a touch of his hand.

He cupped her breast and she leaned into him, winding her arms around his neck and threading her hands into his hair. The silky softness surprised her, as did Jake when he pulled away to tug his sweater off.

Desire thrummed through her veins as she looked at his bare chest, the powerful swell of his arms. She couldn't help herself from touching him, feeling the strength of the muscles beneath his taut skin. He groaned his approval, his mouth claiming hers once more.

He moved closer, the sheet covering her drifting down to tangle with her legs. As his kisses moved to her neck, she was unsure what to do. Should she try and remove the T-shirt she wore or let him do it for her? She'd never had to worry about the next step when kissing a man before; she'd never had the desire to move things beyond that point. She'd done more with Jake than with all the other men she'd dated combined. But now she wished she knew, wished she had the suave assurance of the women he was used to.

She felt her body's response, her breasts growing heavy, her nipples tightening, her sex swelling in hopeful anticipation. His kisses trailed back up her neck, to a spot right behind her ear that made her moan. Jake shifted, propping himself up on an elbow next to her while one hand traveled over her body.

"You have no idea how bad I want you, want you to feel that you're mine, completely." His hand rested between her breasts, the thin cotton no barrier to the heat of him. He traced his thumb around the peak, drawing her nipple tighter without even touching it. Her breath quickened and he pulled the tip between his thumb and finger, making her toes curl into the mattress. "We need to end this game soon. Walking around like this can't be healthy for either of us."

Anxiety niggled at her. Warning bells rang in her mind, yet a part of her she never gave a voice to made her brave. She covered his hand with her own, pressing his palm harder against her breast.

"There is something we could do about that." She lifted her head, kissing his lips softly.

Jake returned her passion, tugging her shirt from below her hips up and over her head. She moved to kiss him again, but he held her back with his hands on her shoulders, his gaze raking over her nakedness like a caress.

"You're absolutely perfect."

In that moment she felt it, beautiful and sexy and bold enough to be like him. To chase down what she wanted until she got it. She reached for the waistband of his jeans, undid the button and slid down the zipper, the back of her hand brushing along the hard ridge of him.

Suddenly, her hands were pinned over her head. Jake's weight was on top of her, his bare chest crushing against her breasts. The thrill of the movement gave her a rush better than any drug she'd ever imagined.

"What do you think you're doing? You can't play with me like this. I only have so much restraint."

She grinned at the quiver in his voice. She'd done that to him, brought him to the edge of control. It should scare her, but it only thrilled. She felt more alive than she ever had. Maybe this was why she'd always been so afraid of him. She'd known he had the power to unlock this part of her she'd kept so carefully hidden. It wasn't him she feared, but her response to him. He'd always made her heart pound and her blood race. A more experienced woman would have known what was happening long ago, but she hadn't known until now with his hard body pressing into hers.

"We can't, Lily. Not now."

"We could." She pulled her lip between her teeth, her bravado faltering as the feelings he'd left her with in the kitchen all those weeks ago came swirling back.

"You hit your head today. I don't want you to wake up tomorrow and think I took advantage of a concussion."

"If you wake up with me I won't."

He shook his head, his dark eyes gleaming. "When I make love to you, Angel, you'll be fully aware of what's happening and why. I want you to look in my eyes and know there is no going back from that moment." He released her hands and rolled off her, leaving her scrambling to cover herself with the sheet. "Now you know why it is such a struggle for me to hold back. I've known we'd be like this from the first time I touched you."

He turned his head, smiling at her as she tried to cover her mortification. Last time he'd rejected her inexperienced advances, this time she must have done something as equally awkward and she didn't even have a clue what it was. Her throat grew tight and hot and she clenched her teeth to keep from giving in to the tears.

"I don't mean to hurt you, Angel. If you would only marry me, I could make you forget all the hurt." Jake's finger traced down her cheek, but she swatted it away.

He didn't understand how marrying him would only hurt her more, how every time she'd give herself to him she'd be reminded of all the women who knew how to please him. There would always be other people in bed with them, getting in the way of what her traitorous heart wanted.

She rolled away from him, wishing she hadn't kissed him, touched him, let him take off the damned shirt. The humiliation of running into the street naked couldn't be as bad as she felt at this moment.

Jake traced his hand over her shoulder, down her back. "You can't hide from me now. I know every inch of your body, how you feel."

"You have no idea how I feel and you never will." She stiffened, drawing strength from somewhere deep inside to protect herself. "Any man with your expertise with women could have made me respond like that."

The bed dipped then rose next to her. "Don't go trying to test that theory, Angel. You'll see a side of me you won't soon forget." Jake's footsteps pounded through the room, and the slamming door echoing in her ears.

Chapter Eight

Jake stood in the doorway between his office and where Lily sat, the fingernails of one hand tapping on the desk as she read through the stack of papers. Her thesis. He knew she had to defend it tomorrow and had made sure to route as much as possible through the Tolliver Enterprises office this week. But he still had designing to do, and his office on this floor was the one set up for that.

Not that he could get much done with Lily here. He'd tried his best to keep busy and not get too close to her ever since the day of her fall, the day he'd almost ruined everything he'd worked so hard for by letting his body run the show. In the last few weeks he'd been careful not to even touch her.

On one hand he hoped his reaction to her would calm down once they were married, but then it also thrilled him to think he'd felt like this about her for over a year. His lips twitched in a grin as he thought about still feeling this way in thirty years.

He glanced down at the printout in his hand. He'd come out to show her the elevation changes on the Clairmont hotel. It amazed him how quickly she'd learned about the firm, how easily she'd taken to scanning designs and finding the flaws. He was so proud of how hard she was working to learn what mattered so much to her father, to him.

If it wasn't for her stupid bargain he would have told her, but he'd only agreed to the deal to give Lily time to learn about herself, to grow in ways he knew she still needed to. He didn't know how other men married younger women without a second thought. He'd been waiting two years for Lily to grow up, and there were only eight years between them.

The phone on her desk rang and he took a step back in case she looked about. He almost turned around and went back to his desk until he heard the name that always raised his blood pressure. Ian. He had half a mind to call the partner of the tool's firm and have him fired. After all, he'd been the one to get the jerk promoted just to get him off of Lily. Now he'd turned up like a bad rash, refusing to go away.

"I can't today. I'm not angry. I've just been busy with work and finishing up my classes. Tomorrow I have to defend—"

Now why would Ian cut her off when she was saying what was obviously most important to her? Lily had been working on her thesis since Jake met her. He didn't have a clue how she pulled all the details from books that she did, but then, he hadn't made the effort to understand what she did the way she had with him. His gut felt like lead at the realization.

"The holiday break is starting, but I'll still be working. And on weekends I'll be doing the admission forms for the doctorate programs at the different universities and looking for an apartment."

That twisted like a knife. She still wanted an apartment, wanted to put things off even longer. And did she mean she was applying to multiple schools? She couldn't be seriously considering leaving the area. Her grades had always been stellar, any school would be crazy not to accept her.

"I can't invite you to the house."

She bloody well better not. He didn't like the idea of Ian near her in restaurants—he wasn't going to allow it in his own house.

"Because Ian, it's not mine. Jake bought the house from my father before he died. He's been letting me live there and work at the firm until I get my feet back under me. After the New Year I'll move into an apartment and I think I'll temp for a while until things are settled about the doctorate program."

Jake leaned his back against the wall and wished she didn't sound so confident about her plans. That was the double-edged sword of giving her time, she was coming into her own. It would mean more when she chose him, but it terrified him that he might have to wait years for that to happen.

"You're being ridiculous and you don't know anything about the situation. Jake didn't coerce my father into anything. The house had to be sold and better it go to him than a stranger. He's been very patient and kind to me since my father became ill. He could have turned me out on the street with nothing, but instead he's made sure I have everything I could possibly need."

He stood up straighter, glad she praised him to someone, even if it was to that idiot of an ex-boyfriend of hers.

"Please. Jake hasn't done any of this to get me into bed. Trust me. He has plenty of company on that front."

He rolled his eyes. She really needed to get past her insecure jealousy. It wasn't attractive, and he wasn't going to spend his life defending himself. He'd watched that tactic destroy his mother and he wasn't about to travel a road he knew was treacherous.

"Ian, really. He stares at everyone. His eyes are so dark it seems like they pierce through you. I'm sure that is what you noticed, not him giving me a second glance. I have to get back to work."

She mumbled a few more times before hanging up. She had a wonderful soft voice, warm and bright. He'd found himself doing this, listening to her conversations far too much lately. It was the easiest way to find things out about her, but it also showed him exactly what she thought of him. Or what she would let people know she thought.

She knew what he felt for her. There couldn't be any doubt in her mind that he'd wanted her since he first saw her, that he'd moved heaven and earth to make sure she was safe. She could have ended the line of questioning from Ian if she'd simply told him they were getting married. But then she didn't seem to have that worked into her plan for the holidays.

The ringing telephone on his desk whipped his head around. He crossed the office quickly, not wanting to make Lily suspicious as to why his calls weren't ringing through her.

"Tolliver." He sat in his chair, spinning around to look out over the skyline.

"It's Ian Landon." The polished voice tried to sound gruff and menacing but failed. "I don't know—"

"I'm sorry, who is this?" Jake grinned, trying not to snicker.

"Ian Landon. I've been dating Lily. I'm sure you know who I am."

"Right, you dated Lily... What was it, two years ago? Short fellow with an oddly flesh-colored beard."

A choked sound came across the line. "I don't care what you're playing at, but I want you to know we've contacted a lawyer."

"The royal we?"

"Lily and I. What you've done is despicable. To take advantage of a dying man, to rob Lily of her home, I won't stand for it. You can't turn her out into the street. I'll be taking her back to Florida with me. After we're married—"

"You are sadly misinformed. I bought the estate for Lily as an engagement present. Lily isn't free to marry as she is already engaged. To me."

Again with the choking sound.

"Not to worry, Liam." Jake smiled wider to keep from laughing. The tool must be twitching with anger at being called the wrong name after such a blow. "We won't be inviting you to the wedding."

Jake rang off, and then stretched his hands behind his head. He was quite proud of himself for not getting angry. Lily might be stringing the boy along, but he knew she had no intention of doing something stupid like marrying that fool Ian. She was too smart for that.

A soft knock on the wall spun him around and out of contemplation. Lily stood just inside his office, her silky blue wrap dress settling invitingly on her curves. He'd been drawn to her beauty at first, but now that he'd grown to be more interested in her wit and spirit it sometimes shocked him how beautiful she was.

"I'm going to grab lunch from the deli. Would you like me to bring you back something?" She tilted her head, her honey blonde hair cascading over her shoulder.

"Maybe I should take you to lunch. Celebrate."

"Did you finish the design for the Clairmont?" She stepped closer to his desk, her gaze scanning the top until it rested on the printout he'd meant to bring her earlier. She picked up the sheet of paper and studied it. "Structurally it's sound enough to remove those wretched columns?"

He looked up at her sparkling eyes, wondering how in the world she'd gone from his ideal woman to absolutely perfect in a few short months.

"The columns were added sixty years ago to make the elevation more ornate."

She pulled a face that made him laugh.

"No accounting for taste. But they can come down, and with the other changes it will look true to period, just earthquake safe."

"You did a wonderful job." She set the paper back on his desk. "Not that I am much of a judge."

His brow furrowed. "You've learned more in the last two months than most do in a year. If I thought you'd be happy here, I'd have you step in as president."

Her eyes widened in shock, then narrowed. "If you are trying to make some kind of deal..."

"No, I wouldn't ask that of you. Just like I need to be able to design here to be happy with the rest of my business, you need to be surrounded by your books and other people who understand what you see in them. It's all too intellectual for me."

"You're an intellectual."

"Business and literary criticism are very different."

She wrinkled her nose. "I'm not a critic."

"What are you then, a theorist?"

She stood a little taller. "That's more accurate, I suppose."

"And you need it to be happy. When do you start your doctoral program?"

She bit her bottom lip and brushed something from the skirt of her dress. "I'm not sure. It depends on the program I can afford."

He stood and rounded the desk to stand next to her. "You know money won't be an issue once we're married."

She looked up at him. "Jake, we're not getting married."

"You don't actually plan on marrying that Ian idiot, do you?"

She released a sharp bark of laughter. "Of course not."

"You might want to tell him that. He just called, accusing me of all sorts of devious acts. Even threatened to sue me."

Her eyes widened. "I'm so sorry. He had no right."

Jake reached out and took her hand. "I know that. But I also told him why I knew you weren't marrying him. But I refuse to invite him to the wedding. On the phone is one thing, but if he actually said something to me in person, I'd have to toss him."

"Jake, were not—"

He tugged her hand, pulling her flush against him. "Not what?"

"Not doing this again, for one thing." She tried to back away, but it only made him hold on tighter.

"This is all either one of us can think about." He slid his mouth against hers, threading a hand through her silken mass of hair. She tried to resist at first, but once he moved his tongue against her full bottom lip her body overrode her defiance and she opened for him.

When he kissed her he could forget that she'd just rejected him again. Her arms around his waist, her hands sliding over his shirt, provided an acceptance that soothed the ache he felt each time she said no. He moved one leg between hers, pressing her as close as he could manage.

"This is so much better without clothes."

Her shocked gasp turned into a smile as he ran his hands over her body, wondering if this dress were really as simple to remove as it looked. If he only tugged on the sash the whole thing would unwrap just like a present.

"Can't you imagine how amazing it would be, Angel? When we're married it could be like this every day, every time."

She wound her hand through his hair, pulling his head down so she could whisper in his ear. "It's a modern world, Jake. We don't have to be married."

"I'm not waiting for the license, Angel. A simple 'yes, I'll marry you' will do." His hand traced along the neckline of the dress, just under the hem so he could feel the top of her breast.

"Jake, are you here?" Dee's voice drifted through the office and Lily stiffened in his arms. She tried to pull away, but he wouldn't let her move as Dee entered the room.

"What have we here?" Dee looked at him with amusement and annoyance. "Is this what you wanted to teach her, Jake? How to make it with the boss in his office? You think that's a life skill she needs to know, or did she know it already?"

Lily swayed at the harsh words but Jake held her firm, wishing she had enough chutzpah to be the one to tell Dee where to put her opinions.

"Dee, if you need to see me you should call first and Lily will set up a time for you. That way you won't interrupt anything important."

"Afternoon delight is important to you?" Dee shook her head, her voice pumped full of contempt. "What is it you think you're doing?"

Lily buried her face in his shoulder, which felt like a sucker punch to his gut. He knew Dee was only looking to protect him, but she needed to stop hurting Lily in the process. "I'm convincing Lily she does in fact want to marry me. If you'll leave, I'd like to get back to it. It did seem to be working for a change."

"Lily, you had better marry him quick, before he sees what you're doing and changes his mind. I hope for both your sakes this is a mess he knows how to clean up." Dee left the room with a flourish, slamming the door behind her.

"Well, that could have gone better." Jake eased his hold on Lily, looking down at her to make sure she wasn't crying. There were no tears, but her entire body was trembling.

"Why do you keep telling people we're getting married? First Ian and now Dee. Why are you doing this?"

"Because we are getting married. Dee is just trying to protect me, and Ian is an idiot. Don't let either of them get to you. But word will get around, so you'll have to get used to people knowing. Not all of them will look down on you for marrying beneath you. There are some who actually think I'm quite the catch."

"So marry one of them. I am not marrying you for a home or for tuition or for sex."

He didn't want her to. But he'd rather die alone than beg her to love him. It would be a cold day in hell before he'd ever admit how he truly felt about her. Once she knew she had that over him, he'd be completely at her mercy and he was never going to be helpless to anyone again.

"You had better take that lunch break now. The thing with marrying beneath you is that the person you're marrying isn't above anything. A minute ago I was done waiting for you to marry me before I made you mine. And I do know you, Lily. If we had made love, then soon enough you would have had a reason to need me. You would never deny your child a father, even one as beneath you as me."

"I have never said that I was better than you. That is all in your head, not mine. But when you act like a caveman ready to pull me around by my hair, I do wonder just what happened to you to make you think so little of yourself."

He took a step toward her, surprised when she didn't move an inch. "You'd better go now, Angel. You wouldn't want me to show you."

"How did it go?"

The deep voice startled Lily and she nearly dropped her book. She turned in the wingback chair, the leather creaking beneath her.

Jake stood in the doorway of the sitting room, his hands in the pockets of his tailored trousers. Even with his shirt unbuttoned and his tie loosened, he still looked perfectly put together. She tried to stretch her lips into a smile, but it just wouldn't come.

"What are you doing here?" She turned around, opening her book again. Really, she should have chosen something more scholarly than the latest attempt at a *Pride & Prejudice* sequel, and she would have if she'd thought she'd be caught. But Jake hadn't been to the house since the incident in the kitchen.

His every footstep reverberated throughout her body. Maybe she needed to have the way he affected her checked out by a medical professional. Just not his girlfriend Susanna. She probably had the same affliction.

"That bad? I was sure you had it nailed." He crouched down beside her chair, his gaze permeating her until she couldn't help but look at him.

"What are you talking about?" With him this close her mind filled with his compelling dark gaze, the firm features of his face, the confident set of his shoulders. There wasn't much room left for thoughts.

"Your thesis. But if it went badly we don't have to talk about it. Next term you won't have to work and you'll kill them."

She blinked, trying to tamp down the warm feeling spreading through her. Whenever Jake was nice to her she wound up doing things that only left her humiliated. But still, it was touching that he cared enough to know she defended her thesis today, that he actually wanted to know how it went.

"The committee seemed impressed. I won't have the final opinion until after the holidays, but they didn't raise any red flags so it should go through."

He reached out and squeezed her knee. "You had me going there. I knew you had it, but you don't seem excited."

"I'm relieved, I think. I'll be excited after the holidays are over and I know where I stand." With everyone, not just the thesis committee at the university.

His warm hand remained on her leg. "Have you given any thought to holiday plans? We could have a party at the house like you've always done."

Her eyes grew gritty at the mere suggestion. Her grief had barely begun to wane. She kept busy to keep from dwelling on how much she missed her father. Now that she only had work to keep her from wallowing in her own thoughts, she didn't know how she was going to make it through.

"Or not. I didn't think you'd be up for it, that's why I hadn't suggested it." He squeezed her knee again and stood. "Next year, maybe."

"It's your house. I'll help with any planning that you

need. It's just that the holidays have always been a sad time for me."

He raised an eyebrow. "I thought you loved Christmas."

She shook her head. "The magic wore off when my mother died. The parties were about keeping occupied so we didn't have too much time to miss her. There's a lot of charity work around the holidays, so I did that too. But this year I'm not exactly on any of the donor lists."

"If you want to be I can make some calls. Once we're married I know you'll be right back at the top of the list. As you should be."

Lily lifted her chin as she looked up at him. "No, I don't want to be under the spotlight this year. It's best that I have my space to figure out the next step." Like how to get him to stop pursuing her, when the idea of distracting him with Dee Gibson now made her physically ill. It was still the best tactic she could think of, but it no longer had the appeal it once did.

He dropped his hands into his pockets. "So what are you thinking of doing for the holidays? It's only a week until the office goes dark."

She gave an evasive shrug, not having an answer. She'd been avoiding thinking about it. Last year she'd been so over-committed she'd barely had a moment to breathe, let alone miss her mother. Her mind flashed on Jake being at nearly every event she'd attended, how he'd even been at the Christmas Eve dinner her father held for his closest friends. Jake had surprised her with a gift, a volume of Jane Austen's letters.

Of course, she hadn't gotten anything for him, and so felt doubly guilty when presented with something so thoughtful. Looking back she felt worse than ever. Yes, he was ruthless and determined, but her reasons for fearing him had nothing to do with Jake. She realized now it all had to do with being afraid of her reaction to him.

She'd treated him terribly, and even after all that he'd done in providing her a refuge from the reporters swirling around a steamy story, and she knew her reputation would have crumbled without his support. If it wasn't for his knack for kissing her stupid and then walking away, she might almost like him. That was what made him so dangerous to her.

The way she lived for his praise and insight wasn't helping matters either. He'd allowed her the ideal set-up to learn about the architecture firm her father and grandfather had loved so much. Now he was practically her mentor, sharing the details of every project so that she knew everything she could think of about the company. People who had treated her with sadness and pity when she first came on board now looked to her for advice and answers. All of it combined to boost her sense of self-worth right out of the gutter.

When she'd made the bargain with Jake she'd wanted to gain skills she could use elsewhere, but what she'd learned most was that she was capable. Of anything she set her mind to. And that was worth far more than the administrative and technical knowledge she'd gained. She'd always appreciate him for that gift.

Jake's warm hand slid beneath her chin, catching her attention. "Why don't you let me take you to dinner to celebrate finishing your degree? I'll even swear off boring you about projects and let you bend my ear about what you plan on theorizing for your doctorate."

"You don't bore me with the projects." She swallowed hard and stared down at the book in her lap. Her father had always thought advanced degrees were a waste of time since she'd likely be a society wife with nothing more to do than plan parties and debate spa treatments. Every man she'd ever dated had emphatically agreed she was wasting her time with school. But from the first time she'd met him, Jake had always been supportive of her education, even defending her choices a time or two when others thought it whimsical and romantic that she studied at all.

Maybe the void of being finished with school this term was getting to her, or she had some kind of residual head injury from the fall. Right this moment she wanted to wrap her arms around Jake Tolliver's neck and thank him. Thank him for being a shelter in the storm these last few months, for believing her more than the beautiful twit most wrote her off as. Really, this sense of admiration and gratitude was dangerous when blended with the hum of attraction she always felt around him.

"Talk about the buildings doesn't bore you because you understand it. Believe me, it can send other people into a coma."

Lily forced a weak smile, thinking he must be referring to Dee. Lucky for her, the reminder of his other

149

women was just the ice water she needed to wake herself up.

"I'm not in the mood for dinner. Thank you for thinking of me, but I'm staying in."

He shrugged. "I'll see what Emmaline can whip up for us." He stepped behind her toward the door. She spun in her chair.

"No, don't. She's going out tonight and I told her not to bother with anything. She'll cancel if you ask anything of her."

"Cancel what?"

Lily couldn't help but grin. "Her date. John from the landscaping service. He's been after her forever. I finally talked her into it."

"Quite the matchmaker, aren't you?"

"She deserves to be happy. She's been so down since my father's illness. Anything is better than moping around here."

"Isn't that what you're doing?"

With a sigh, she returned her attention to the book. She didn't want to argue with him, not when it had ended so volatile last time.

She re-read the same page three times, waiting to hear the front door slam closed. Instead, she felt her hair move, his fingers playing in the strands behind her.

"I'm sorry if that came out harsh. But who's going to be honest with you if I'm not, Lily?"

Who indeed. He was honest, brutally so even when it

hurt. But she couldn't answer. Her emotions were in such a swirl she was afraid opening her mouth would cause the façade to crack and he'd see she'd begun to soften toward him. She couldn't see a future without him in it, which scared her more than she'd ever admit. She had to make a break soon, or she'd give in to him more than physically.

"I don't think you should be in the house for Christmas. Not this year."

She nodded, having considered getting away as a balm to soothe the ache of missing her parents. But she couldn't afford to use any of her savings for a vacation when she needed every penny to get an apartment.

"We should spend the holidays together." He said the words tentatively, as if testing the waters.

She shook her head. "I can't do the party circuit this year. I just don't have it in me to smile and hug all those people who've ignored me these last few months. And staying in town wouldn't be much better than staying here." Besides, if she stayed here she could pack what she'd be taking to her new apartment and decide which pieces of jewelry she'd have to sell to be able to afford to live on her own.

"I hate the parties too. The only ones I ever liked were the ones here."

"It is a wonderful house for entertaining. It's no wonder why you were so willing to buy it."

He came around the chair, again crouching so his intent gaze pierced through her. "I bought it for you, Lily.

You know I am absolutely infatuated with you."

The smile creeping across his handsome face was completely disarming. She struggled with resisting him whenever he was kind. Showing it would give him the key to breaking down all her defenses.

Lily swallowed hard and cut her gaze back to the book. "Don't let Dee hear you say that. She might have let you get away with it once, but I doubt she'll put up with it again."

He shook his head regretfully. "Stop trying to put Dee between us. It doesn't work."

"Just because it'd be your ideal situation doesn't mean it doesn't bother me."

"It shouldn't. From the first time I touched you, I haven't been able to think of anyone else. You consume me completely, and the more I learn about you the more I know my instincts about us were right. I won't act the fool for you, Lily, but I certainly feel it often enough."

She rolled her bottom lip in, her teeth pulling at the flesh. How many ways could she explain to him that she couldn't be anything but miserable in the situation he was offering? He wanted a well-brought-up trophy wife on his arm at events who would give his children a history he couldn't. She could never look anyone in the eye knowing she was nothing but a decorative brood mare. And she certainly wouldn't bring a child into the world in such an unstable home.

"I don't want you to decide now, but I don't want to stay in town either. Before I met you I spent Christmases in Hawaii with my grandmother. She'll love you, I promise. I'd bring her here, but she can't stand the cold. It's a complete change of scenery. I think it would really help you get through."

She hoped her smile was noncommittal. "It would give you the wrong idea. If I go with you, you'll think I'm agreeing to marry you and I can't."

He took both her hands in his own, a warm sensation traveling through her body as he smiled gently. "Do you know how long it has been since I've said please?"

Her eyes grew heavy, so she blinked away the sensation in order to gain control. "Is that what I am supposed to tattle to your grandmother about?"

Chapter Nine

Jake felt all of his troubles drift away as his plane left the ground. Lily was here beside him, on a trip he'd wanted to take her on since the moment he met her. He wasn't about to let her spend the holidays alone, and he didn't want for his grandmother to have to do the same either. He was managing to make both the women in his life happy at once. He knew better than to think it would happen often. Still, it made him feel like the cat that swallowed the canary.

"Most people get anxious at take-off. Did you take something?" Lily asked.

"Nope, this is all you." He reached across the plush chairs and squeezed her hand. It amazed him how much closer he felt to her now than he had three months ago. Giving her the space to find her way to him had been a gamble, but she was coming around. Once he got her all the way, she'd never leave. A rush of excitement thrummed through him and he tried to bring himself back down to earth.

She didn't love him, and she probably never would. He hoped that in time and with the children her affection for him would grow and she might forget her initial distaste for his company. But she was growing to like him, and that was enough for now. That, coupled with the fiery passion sizzling between them, would be enough, more than most people ever got.

Lily still held all the cards though. He hated not having the upper hand in anything. He wanted to explain to her about Dee, even her ridiculous notions about Susanna, but he didn't want to set a precedent where he'd have to defend himself every time she saw him with another woman. His mother had spent her life trying to justify herself to his father and never could. Lily would have to learn to trust him or deal with her own insecurities. Maybe once she agreed to marry him he might explain. Once.

He didn't want to think about anything negative. They were on holiday after all, and that included a break from worrying about their future.

He cleared his throat. "Have you been to Hawaii?"

She shook her head. "Dad preferred the Caribbean."

"It's amazing. A few short hours in the air and it's like being in another world."

"Have you always gone there?"

His shoulders tensed when he thought of the first time he'd arrived in the islands. "Only since my mother died."

Lily's brows knit together. "Where did your grandmother live before?"

"She hasn't left the islands in about thirty years. It

was my mother who left." He shifted in his seat, knowing he'd never get comfortable while talking about this but realizing that if he didn't tell Lily, his grandmother would. "My mother was very young when she met my father. He was a fisherman who didn't care that she was seventeen. But then he never cared about much beyond himself.

"When they found out she was pregnant he spirited her away to Alaska. No one in her family heard from her again, they didn't even know about me until I came to tell them their daughter was dead.

"I was angry and wanted some kind of retribution for how they'd abandoned her, how they'd never come to save us. But they didn't know. They'd looked for her, but the trail stopped dead in Alaska. He was only able to keep jobs in short jumps so they moved a lot. Alaska for crab and cod, Washington for salmon and sturgeon, halibut and tuna in Oregon. When I started school we settled in the city and he'd be gone for stretches. She could have left him then. I don't understand why she never did."

He waited for the pity, for the more probing questions he'd have to refuse to answer, but they never came. Lily merely squeezed his hand, rubbing her thumb over his.

"Your grandmother must have been comforted to see you, even though it was a shock."

"I don't know if it was at first. I look an awful lot like the man who took her daughter. But she welcomed me from the beginning, even when I was resentful and hostile. It didn't take long for me to warm to her though. She looks like my mother, and when we first met I took comfort in that."

"It sounds like the two of you have quite a bond now. I hope I won't be interfering with your time together. I don't want to intrude."

"You couldn't. She's been expecting you for a year."

"Why would she do that?"

"Because I told her that I'd met the woman I was going to marry. She's been after me to bring you to her ever since. Though when I said you were finally coming she did have a talk with me about the propriety of maintaining separate bedrooms while under her roof. If it wasn't so funny, it would have been mortifying."

Lily's eyes widened. "We can't share a room. Even at the penthouse you've never—"

"Calm down, Angel. If I only wanted you in my bed you'd have been there by now. I have too much respect for you to put you in a situation like that." Not that he hadn't come damned close to losing control once or twice, but he wouldn't let it happen again.

"I don't know if I believe you, but I'm hoping my bedroom door has a lock."

"With the way you behave, I should be the one who needs protecting."

She pulled her hand from his to whack him in the chest. Thanks to the smile on her face he had to grin back.

He took her hand again, resting it on his thigh. "I'm glad you decided to come, Lily. I've spent so much time with you lately I don't know what I'd do without you to talk to. I'd always want you around, except I think about you naked every two minutes and I'd accomplish nothing all day and you'd never have a moment's peace."

Lily chuckled and leaned back in her seat, as relaxed as he'd seen her in months. His chest swelled with pride that he'd been the one to relieve some of her tension. If only she'd let him take it all away.

First class had always been good enough before, but Lily could get used to flying on a private jet. The privacy and quiet took all the stress out of traveling during the holiday season. As they stepped off the plane the humid air wrapped around her like a hug, the sun shining on her face.

The warmth relaxed her completely, her last vestiges of doubt about whether she should have come disappearing. She saw him reaching for her hand as they walked from the tarmac toward a waiting car. Before, she would have either ignored the gesture or hidden her hands behind her back. He'd been a dream on the plane and had taken her to paradise, so she slipped her fingers against his.

The whole trip she'd been thinking of what life would be like if she'd never known him or if he hadn't been so determined to have her. The problems her father had would still have wreaked havoc on her life, but the aftermath would have been much messier.

Her home would have been sold to strangers, her

degree forgotten, everything she would have managed to salvage would have been sold to support herself while she found a job that had no possibility of supporting her. Because of Jake and his kindness she'd been allowed to grieve in the only home she'd ever known, finished her masters, gained marketable job skills and found a friend. A real one.

He was honest with what he wanted, and so was she. Still, he'd built up her confidence, given her a chance to learn the business her father had created, and helped her find an enthusiasm that lived within. It made her happy not to have to share him with other women for a while, his grandmother notwithstanding. It would give him a chance to see a life without his string of mistresses, because Lily found herself on the verge of loving him, nearly agreeing to his proposal. She was almost to the point of wishing he would have some epiphany and decide he didn't need the other women, just her. But she knew it was far more likely that being together now would be the bittersweet end she needed in order to move on. Hopefully to a university across the country where she wouldn't have to be constantly reminded of his amorous exploits.

As she slid into the waiting red convertible, it was hard to believe the man starting the car wasn't as perfect as he seemed. She took a deep breath, pulling the spiced scent of tropical blooms into her lungs and letting go of the worry. Reality would be there when they got back home, like the cold wind of winter.

The sun was low in the sky as they left the airport, painting everything with a golden glow. Lily loved the feel of the breeze through her hair as Jake maneuvered the car out of the relative normalcy of the airport area into the unknown of what seemed to be a winding road through a jungle.

In a few minutes they were high above it all, able to look out at the ocean and down on the colorful vegetation embracing the island. He made a few more turns, and then pulled into a secluded area with a view of everything. Lily took it all in, from the tall palm trees swaying in the breeze to the turquoise blue of the pacific gently kissing the caramel-colored sand of the beach and the flowers sparkling like jewels on the lush plants.

She turned to ask Jake what his grandmother's house was like, but found him staring at her intently. She tilted her head in question which only made him smile.

"I need a favor and I'm not used to asking for them. Usually people owe me a favor and I collect, not the other way around."

"Within reason, I think it's safe to say I probably owe you one." Or seventeen. But since he wasn't counting she wasn't about to get out a tally sheet.

He let out a deep breath and released his choke hold on the steering wheel. "My grandmother isn't as healthy as she seems. She'll put on a brave face while we're here and then take weeks to recover. I have a nurse who lives with her full-time to monitor her diabetes and her heart." His lips twisted in a wistful grin. "I still find it hard to believe there is anything wrong with having a heart that's too big. But anyway, this could very well be her last

Christmas. I hope not, but I am realistic about her condition."

Lily reached her hand to his arm and rested it there. Jake took her hand in his, bringing it to his lips and kissing it in a gesture so tender it made her insides melt. He held her hand tightly between them and looked right at her, his gaze intense in a different way than she was accustomed to.

"I will marry you, Lily Harris, the moment you are ready. I know you're not there yet, but I want you to let her believe the wedding is imminent."

She tried to pull her hand away, but he held it firmly. "Jake, lying to her is not a good idea."

"It's not a lie. We're inevitable. I know if you don't do this and we lose her before we're married you'll wish you had. She worries about me. The same pictures you've seen in the magazines, she has too. She's not as keen on believing the stories, but I know she wants more for me than that garbage."

"She wouldn't want you to lie to her."

"What if I extended our agreement? You can stay on at Tolliver-Harris and stay at home as long as you need. I'll forget the New Year's timeline. You do this for me, and we'll do everything else at your pace." His eyes were filled with a curious, profound longing, as if he were actually pleading for more than he was asking.

"I appreciate all you've done, but I'm ready for the game to be over. I won't deny that we're attracted to one another, but I won't live your life."

"Because you will never trust me." Raw hurt glittered in his eyes.

She gave a shrug, pulling her bottom lip between her teeth. "Because I deserve more than being someone's socially acceptable trophy wife." It tugged at her that it was Jake who taught her that lesson, perhaps a bit too well for his own gain.

"I agree, but that has nothing to do with what I am asking." He pulled out a black box from his pocket and opened it. A vintage art-deco filigree engagement ring blinked up at her. The detail of the delicate setting made her want to take a closer look, but she didn't dare. "The ring was hers. She gave it to me last year to give to you, only when I told your father he wasn't so keen on the idea. If you don't like the ring you can pick out your own, any one you want when we do get married. But I am asking you to wear this ring here. I would love for her not to worry about me anymore."

Lily rubbed her face with her hands, wishing there were an easy solution to this. "What am I supposed to do? Lie to a dying woman to give her peace? You have me up against a wall here."

A devilish look lightened his dark gaze. "I've never had you up against a wall, but I think I'd like to."

The sensual image flashed in her mind and her body warmed at the thought. "Would you stop?"

"Why, does it scare you to know exactly what I want from you?" He gave her body a raking gaze. "Are you still afraid of me, Lily?"

She shook her head. "I never really was." What terrified her was her own reaction to him, her longing for him.

"When I first told you that I wanted to marry you, you claimed you hated me. Did you mean it?"

The opportunity to free herself from him was right there, tied up with a golden bow. If he'd stayed the enigmatic stranger she would have been able to lie and end things once and for all. But he was her friend now, and even if he had his own agenda, he'd been the only one who'd been there for her when she'd needed a friend.

"I hated how helpless I was at that moment, and that I'd let myself get there. It wasn't you I hated really, but that you never would have allowed yourself to be in such a position. It felt as if I were trapped and drowning at the same time. You tried to save me, and when I refused you taught me how to save myself. For that I'll always be grateful."

"So you'll do it?" His eyes held a laughter she wished he'd release.

She nodded, watching as he took her hand and slid the ring on her finger. "If she is in perfect health I may have to confess the entire ruse. Just so you know."

"Now you have me up against a wall. I'd like to have her healthy and you wearing the ring." He kissed her hand again and then released it. "Do you like it? It's so refined and classic I thought it suited you."

She looked down at the ring, realizing she could stare at it for hours. Everything suddenly felt very real. They were overlooking the ocean in the middle of a tropical paradise and the man she was in love with had just put a beautiful ring on her hand. If only the happy ending came with this fairy tale. She knew she could have the impression of a marriage with Jake, but it would never go deeper than the façade. He had no intention of loving anyone, or ending his collection of new lovers. Two reasons why she couldn't possibly give in.

Jake's thumb brushed over her cheek, the dampness of a tear cooling against her skin. "I always thought you'd cry when we got engaged."

"We're not." She sat up straight and squared her shoulders. "This is just for your grandmother."

"It doesn't have to be." His husky whisper wove around her, but she wouldn't let herself be caught in the snare.

"I'm not interested, thank you." Her words were heavy with sarcasm.

"Liar. You think about it constantly. You know as well as I do it's not a matter of if, but of when. You will be my wife, Angel."

She turned to him to object, but the words never left her mouth because his lips were there first. Her body responded on instinct, wanting to open for him, to taste him. Somewhere deep inside she found what was left of her backbone and used it to put her hands firmly against his chest and push.

"We're not doing this again. You get me worked up to the point where I'm willing to be with you and then you reject me and run to one of your girlfriends. They aren't around, are they? Did you pack one of them along?"

"With all I've given you I'd think you'd be over petty jealousy." He started the car and revved the engine.

"I'm not jealous, just practical. You don't want me and they aren't here. I wouldn't want you to go to all the trouble of having to find someone new."

"Jealousy is an emotion you don't wear well, Angel. I suggest you get rid of it."

"I'm not jealous. That would mean I was in love with you, and I know better than that."

"Yes, we both know better, don't we?" He put the car in reverse so forcefully she was jerked forward in her seat, holding the armrest as he made his way back onto the winding road.

"What will you do when we get home and I leave?" She asked over the roar of the road. "I've kept my side of the deal. I know the business better than I ever thought I would, so I'm free to go."

"You'll never be free of me, Lily. Try and run, you'll find that out."

Coldness washed over his features, the familiar countenance of a man in control of the world slipping over him. It chilled her to know something ominous would happen if she left, and he wouldn't have to do a thing. Just as her heart tore a little when he sealed himself off like this, it would break completely when she had to leave him.

Opponents, not allies. Lily hated how a single conversation could turn how she and Jake reacted to one another around. Some people worried about walking on eggshells, but she and Jake lived with bare feet on broken glass.

She followed him past the grassy drive where they'd parked to the entry of the house hidden beneath the graceful bamboo. Being here was like walking through a kaleidoscope, with purple bell-shaped flowers on one side and pale blooms that looked like stars on the other. Tiny yellow birds fluttered about a bush with red blossoms as big as dinner plates.

An elderly woman pulled open the door, her pale face brightening as she reached for Jake. She was nothing like what Lily had been envisioning. Jake talked of his background as being so poor and such a struggle she never imagined his family would have had any other life.

As soon as she saw the woman, Lily knew the opulence of the house was intrinsic to her and not something Jake had provided once he'd become successful. There was nothing about her that was oppressed or ill-used. She looked just like the grand dames of the charity set Lily had been so used to, the kind of woman her own grandmothers would have been had they lived long enough for her to have known them.

The glassy dark gaze turned from Jake to Lily as a wide smile caused her wrinkles to deepen. "My goodness, Lilianna. You are even more beautiful than Jakob claimed. I'm glad you could join us this year, though I wish it were for a better reason. The first holiday season after a loss is always hard. At least you're still with family."

Lily blushed and twisted the ring on her finger. Maybe for the few days she was here she'd let this woman be her family. It certainly felt like the right thing to do.

Jake's arm snaked around her shoulders. "Angel, meet my grandmother, Thalia. She seems to have adopted you already."

"Of course I have. I've been waiting for far too long for someone to bring you to your senses."

"Nana, let's not pressure Lily to have to do the impossible."

Thalia waved her thin hand through the air as she walked deeper into the house. "There's a ring on her finger, so I think she is quite capable of what many thought unattainable."

Under any other circumstances Lily might have laughed at the compliment. But it only served to remind her how Dee Gibson would likely give her closet of designer shoes to be standing on the polished concrete floor next to Jake.

They followed Thalia past the entry to where the house opened up and became a windowed showcase of all the island had to offer. Lily wandered past the comfortable Balinese furnishings to stare at the view of the ocean below. A path seemed to start at one end of thick vegetation and end at the horseshoe beach. As tired as she was after a day of traveling, she wanted to explore, to surround herself with the tropical elegance around her until she couldn't think about all she'd lost, and what she was about to.

"Lilianna." The frail fingers on her arm turned her attention back to the other occupants of the room, which seemed to have increased by one tall, exotic beauty while she'd been enthralled with the scenery. "This is my nurse, Mikayla. She stays here with me to keep Jakob from worrying."

Lily put on a smile as she was forced to watch the beauty embrace Jake, squeezing him with more than familial comfort. He'd been coming here for years, coming to her. Lily's blood iced in her veins. She'd been looking forward to not sharing him for a while, and all along he'd known he still had his piece on the side.

Thalia linked her arm with Lily, waiting for Mikayla to let go of Jake and turn to them. "Lilianna and Jakob are getting married, soon I hope. Isn't she stunning? And she's never been to the island. Jakob will be quite busy making sure she loves it here. That way I know they'll visit often."

"Of course they will." Mikayla passed her discerning gaze over Lily, making her feel as if she were up for auction and found overpriced. "Jake, why don't I catch you up on how things are going here while Lily settles in?"

Lily blinked at the dismissal, looking to Jake who seemed to agree that she should be sent to her room and kept out of the way for his reunion with yet another lover. A minute ago she'd been glad she came, but now she wondered why she'd bothered when nothing would ever change.

Thalia showed her to a cozy bedroom with another amazing view of the tropical foliage and a bed covered with oversized pillows. It looked so lush and inviting she nearly dove in, wanting to cover herself and hide away.

"I can't tell you how happy I am to have you here." Thalia took both Lily's hands in her own. "You're all Jakob ever talks about and I can tell just from meeting you how much you've changed his life. After all he's been through, he deserves the kind of happiness only finding love can bring." She squeezed Lily's hands and then released them. "Once you've settled in I'd like for us to sit down and have a chat. I know Jakob wants you to himself, but we'll carve out some time."

Lily held her smile until Thalia left her alone, and then regret washed over her. She turned to the window, only to see the reason why. Jake and Mikayla were laughing on the corner of the lanai, her hand on his arm. Her heart ached as she thought of how rarely Jake laughed with her. And when he did, they usually wound up fighting anyway.

She stepped back and sat on the bed, hating how jealousy consumed her. She couldn't live like this, she'd surely go mad. She wanted to run, but pride had her wondering if it might not feel better to take him from one of his mistresses for once, rather than fading into the background the way she had for the others. Maybe if he were sleeping with her, he might stop always finding it elsewhere.

"Are you tired, Angel?" Jake came into the room, rolling her bag behind him.

Lily didn't reply, still toying with what her next move would be.

"What do you think of my grandmother?"

"She is definitely your greatest asset." Lily turned one knee on the bed so she faced Jake.

"For now." He joined her on the bed, his leg brushing hers.

"Did you get what you needed from Mikayla?"

His eyes narrowed. "It wasn't the best news, but it's what I expected. Do you want a detailed report?"

She shook her head, hating to think of what he might say.

"Good, because there is something I need to do."

She expected him to get up, but instead he leaned forward and surprised her with a chaste kiss. He pulled back with a smile, but she wasn't ready to lose his attention yet. Placing her hands on either side of his face, she pulled him to her. She tasted his lips, smiling as he opened for her and slipped his hands around her waist. She leaned into the kiss, deepening it as her hands drifted down his body, her palms resting over his racing heart.

"There you are, Jake."

They broke apart to see Mikayla standing in the open door. Lily kept her hands where they were, not wanting to cower the way she had when Dee had broken in on them.

"Do you want me to take your bags to the bungalow?"

Mikayla asked as if she hadn't just interrupted. "I could help you unpack."

"I'll take care of anything he needs, thanks." Lily said, plastering on her best debutant smile.

"Okay. Jake, if you need anything else, you just let me know." The woman wiggled her fingers in a wave before she finally left.

"If you weren't so damned sexy when you're jealous, I might tell you to knock it off." He tried to kiss her again, but Lily stood up and crossed the room to close the door.

"You don't stay in the house?"

He shook his head. "I designed a bungalow a few years back. Want to see it?"

"Did you build it so you'd have more privacy with your Amazon friend? You have a woman everywhere you go, don't you?"

The cold veneer washed over him once more and he sighed. "You should write books instead of reading them. You have an amazing imagination. I'm not going to be rude to Mikayla just to make you happy. I trust her with my grandmother, and I don't do that lightly."

"You talked me into coming and into wearing your ring so your grandmother and I could have a better Christmas. If I catch you with Mikayla, I'll tell Thalia everything. Absolutely everything. Won't she be proud of you then?"

Jake stood and walked past her, not even pausing as he walked through the door and out of the house.

Chapter Ten

Dinner was short and terse. Thalia might be frail, but she wasn't stupid, and Jake knew she sensed the tension. They both knew Mikayla liked him more than she should, they'd even talked about it before, but it was Lily's taut reaction whenever Mikayla tried to speak to him that had Thalia narrowing her shrewd eyes in a way he knew was an order for him to solve the problem. He wasn't at all surprised when she claimed a headache and asked Mikayla to help her to bed.

Lily rose to do the same, but he grabbed her hand. "Let me show you the beach."

"It's getting late, it will be dark soon." She blinked her big brown doe eyes at him, almost petulant in her excuse.

"There's a full moon. We'll be fine." He tugged her off the veranda and onto the grass before she could launch further protests. If she wanted to have it out with him, she could do it on the beach, not in his grandmother's home.

He found the path leading down to the secluded strip of shoreline with ease, guiding her through the dark ferns and overhanging branches of the koa trees. She kept pace with him, so he didn't stop until he kicked off his sandals and dug his toes into the still-warm sand.

Lily stepped away from him, staring at the ocean as the white sand glistened in the waning light. The gentle waves lapped at the sand, the white foam decorating the shoreline like lace. The moon lit the crests of the surf, making them glitter an eerie silver. Above them the stars studded a velvet sky.

Jake stood behind her and wrapped his arms about her waist, not letting go when she stiffened. "She thinks we need time to make up. We can't go back right away. We should do something to pass the time."

"Mikayla is the kind of woman you do to pass the time, not me. You should have asked her."

"If I wanted her, I would have." He rested his chin on her shoulder. "Do you really think I would do that to you?"

"Of course you would."

"I know that you believe that up here." He tucked her hair behind her ear and then nipped at the lobe. "But what about here?" His palm cupped her breast, able to feel her heart pounding beneath his hand.

"You and all your women won't fit in there." She tried to wrestle herself free, so he used the momentum to spin her around in his arms.

"What if it's just me?"

"It never has been, it never will be, and I'll never be able to live with it, no matter how much money and power you have."

"I'm telling you, it's just me."

She raised her chin, assuming the regal dignity he usually admired. "And I'm telling you, I have eyes. I've watched you tell people what they need to hear at work to make a deal. I've watched the way women look at you, the way they look at me like some stupid twit because I can't possibly know what you do with them when I'm not around. Except I do know."

"You don't even hear me. When are you going to listen?" He frowned in complete exasperation. What would it take to get through to her?

"Me? I've been telling you for months that I won't marry you, and today you put a ring on my finger."

He shook his head. "You're not listening to yourself. If you would just get past the jealousy things would be so much easier."

"For you!" She twisted herself free and stalked backwards, away from him. "Do you think about how this would be for me at all?"

"All I do is think of you." He pushed a hand through his hair, trying to come up with something, anything to make her believe him. And failing. He never failed.

"Then how can you ask me to live like that? Is it some kind of thrill for you, to see how low you can bring me? My father may have lost our money and our standing, but nothing you do will cause me to lose myself." Her brown eyes glowed with a savage inner fire.

She tried to flee, but he caught her by the arm.

"I recall a few times when you nearly lost yourself,

were more than willing in my arms."

"That was just sex, Jake. Surely you know all about that. Isn't that why you have so many women? You didn't think your prowess had to do with anything more than experience, did you?"

He pushed her arm away from him and let her go, reeling back as if she'd hit him with far more than words. Perhaps Dee had been right all along and Lily had been playing him for a fool. His instincts had never been so wrong. He watched her start back up the path to the house, but he didn't follow.

Instead, he turned back to the surf and sat down, letting the water play at his feet. He still wanted her, wanted her to see him as worthy and capable, and he hated himself for not being able to walk away. He should, but he'd been trapped by the same emotional minefield that had ensnared his mother and stifled Will Harris. He tried not to, really put every effort into not loving her, into keeping her an obsession, but now he was stuck beneath the weight of his own want, with nothing to ease the burden.

He knew better than to try to appease her each time she flew into a jealous snit. It never worked. Each rage would only intensify until one day he'd be as defeated as his mother had been. Yet he knew living without Lily was impossible. He'd seen how Will had tried to move through life without Lily's mother, and had sunk into a life where nothing could fill the gaping hole left in his heart.

Jake wanted a different life than the trap his mother

had been snared in. He wanted a real family, but for the life of him he couldn't see that without Lily. Until he met her, children had always been an abstract thought, but now they had her dreamy smile and soulful eyes. He didn't know if he could trust another woman to have his child. If he turned into the kind of father his had been, he needed a woman strong enough to leave him. That left him alone, mourning the loss of a woman he never had.

There had to be a better way, but for the life of him he couldn't see it.

Rays of morning sunlight warmed her face and Lily woke to a new morning. As her eyes came into focus she gasped, pulling the sheets around her. Jake sat next to her on the bed, his face set in a grim scowl.

"Did you cry yourself to sleep for me or because of me?"

Lily pressed her hands to her eyes, indeed finding the telling puffiness. Last night had been horrid, her worst nightmare come to life. He'd brought her all the way here, had her feeling that there might be a chance for them to be happy together, and then swept it all away when she found he had a woman everywhere he went.

Last night he'd tried to finesse her the way he did a business deal and she'd nearly succumbed. Somehow she'd found the strength to stand up for herself, but in so doing she'd seen how deeply her words had cut him. Her eyes grew heavy now just thinking about the look on his face.

"I have some gifts to deliver to the families who help look after my grandmother. Mikayla is leaving with me, so if you need anything you'll have to fend for yourself."

She took her hands away from her eyes, wondering why he would rub salt in the wound like that. To tell her he was taking his mistress out on Christmas morning was completely unnecessary, unless he was trying to punish her for last night. She supposed she should be grateful he'd at least heard her when she threatened to tell his grandmother everything if she had to watch him and Mikayla together.

Lily sat up, watching him as he stood. "What have you told Thalia? I don't want us to have conflicting stories."

He shook his head, his hand resting on the doorknob. "I'm telling the truth, Lily. I wish you knew how to listen to it."

She wanted to ask which truth, but he was already gone. As she showered and changed, she wished she could think of something besides Jake and Mikayla sharing a passionate embrace deep within the jungle.

The image sickened her. She didn't understand why there was no room in her mind for any other man, and yet he could have a different woman in his bed every night and not think anything was wrong with that. It might be the fundamental difference between men and women, but she couldn't let that be an excuse.

She hated herself for hurting him, even in self-preservation. She hated him for being wonderful one moment and dreadful the next. It was such an unhealthy place to be in, she made up her mind to move out of the house as soon as she got back. The reprieve he'd offered in exchange for wearing the ring would only make matters worse. They had to cut their losses now before any more damage was done.

She wondered what he'd tell Thalia when everything was over. Lily had always wanted a grandmother, wanted someone older and wiser to confide it. She didn't want to become too attached to Thalia, but it felt wrong to brood in her room while the older woman was alone, so Lily went in search of her.

Thalia sat in a plush chair on the veranda, the rays of sunlight filtering through the leaves overhead that shaded her from the heat. She looked up from her book as Lily stepped outside.

"Are you all right, dear? Jakob said you weren't feeling yourself this morning." Her pale face drooped with worry.

"Just a little jet lag, I think. Fresh air is the best thing for that, don't you agree?" Lily gave her best smile and took the seat next to the elderly woman.

"Of course. Jakob was concerned, but he is prone to worry, always trying to be responsible for everyone. You'll have to help him make sure he looks after himself. He's always so busy trying to lay the world flat for his friends. He winds up climbing every mountain alone."

Lily wasn't sure what to say to such a glowing opinion of Jake. "He was very kind to me when my father passed.

I don't like to think of what it would have been like if he hadn't been there."

"Of course he would be there for you. I'm so thankful that you're with him, dear. He is wonderful, but only once you get past the moat of vulnerability that surrounds him. It's to be expected after the childhood he had to endure. It's a testament to you that he's been able to overcome it. I always worried he'd never be able to admit his love for anyone after the way he grew up, and no woman who loved him would be able to suffer through that. It says so much about your character that he's been able to trust you."

Lily's throat tightened at the words. Thalia was so warm and welcoming, she wanted to throw herself at the older woman's feet and confess everything that had happened the last few months, to see if a lifetime of experience saw a better end than she did. But this was Jake's grandmother, and likely to see everything he did through rose-colored glasses.

She cleared her throat, hoping she wouldn't sound strained. "Jake told me about his mother. He said finding you has been a comfort to him now that she's gone."

Thalia smiled, her pale cheeks warming to a rosy pink. "I'm glad. I only wish we could have done more for our Rebecca, and for Jakob. It was a hard life for them and I think her pride must have kept her from coming home. It was hard to forgive her for what she put him through. As a mother, I don't understand how she could stay with a man who would be so cruel to her child. There is a limit to what love allows, you know?"

179

Lily nodded, her image of Jake changing in her mind. She'd known his childhood hadn't been easy, but she hadn't imagined the depth of darkness Thalia hinted at.

"I suppose in the end justice was served. I think Jakob should have let the beast rot in a state hospital, but after the accident he moved him to the finest care facility he found. I couldn't do it. I don't understand why someone who routinely beat his son for defending his mother is allowed to live, even as a vegetable. It's amazing how someone whose parents were so awful can still be a good son."

Lily blinked, recalling how Jake had said he wished his father were dead. Their history explained why, though it didn't account for why he made sure the man was cared for now. Shouldering responsibility was so ingrained in him he'd take care of a man who'd had no regard for him even as a child.

"My daughter must have done something right as a mother for him to be such a champion to so many. All those girls from his old neighborhood that he supported through school or helped get set up in business have been his way of keeping them from the fate his mother suffered. Every new job she got, that man accused her of having an affair. I wish she would have, maybe then she would have found the strength to leave him."

"Situations like that can be so complicated," Lily offered, unsure what to say. It was hard to think of anything but a tiny dark-eyed boy trying to stand up to a grown man. He'd had to learn as a child the injustice of the world, had to see his mother punished for crimes she didn't commit, had to shut down parts of himself to get through the abuse. It was no wonder he could throw a wall down around his emotions. He'd been doing it all his life.

Thalia nodded. "Jakob likes to say it's important for a woman to know she can take care of herself so she doesn't feel trapped with a man she needs to escape. It's very forward thinking of him. We fought for that in my generation, so it makes me proud that he lives the change."

Was that why he'd given her time to finish her degree and learn to work these last few months? She'd felt ensnared, but he was the one who'd made sure she knew what to do if she cut herself free.

"Oh dear, I've distressed you with all this. I shouldn't have started."

Lily shook her head, blinking back the tears prickling her eyes. "It's not you, honestly."

"He's still holding back from you. He hasn't told you he loves you, has he?"

She shook her head again, letting out a slow breath and reining in her emotions. "He wants a life with me."

"He loves you, dear. I promise. Sometimes with very strong men it is hard for them to risk sharing how they feel, especially if they are unsure you feel the same."

"But I—"

"You love him, I know. There was some advice my mother gave me once that kept me going through my marriage. She said that a successful man can make you believe anything he says, but if you want to know if that man actually loves you, you look at how he treats you and not at the words he uses."

Lily smiled, having never received any motherly pearls of wisdom before. She had to admit that his harsh words aside, Jake treated her like a princess. Still, she wondered how he treated his other women. She understood so much now, even his need to have many women love him. The one woman who should have loved him enough to protect him hadn't, and so the love of one woman would never be enough to make up for that.

"Thank you for the advice." Her chest tightened as the need to unburden herself swelled inside. "Jake wants things that I want, but there are people who will get in the way of that. I mean, right now he's gone off with Mikayla to do—"

The older woman's brows knit together. "No, he didn't. He took her to her parents' house on his way to run errands. She's already called to tell me his mood had not improved any and he'd simply dropped her at the door."

Lily tilted her head to the side, unsure what to think. Maybe his grandmother sensed trouble and wanted to cover for him. Still, a part of her hoped the older woman was right. Learning that Jake helped out women from the neighborhood might be able to explain away his relationship with Susanna as well, but nothing could rationalize Dee Gibson.

Before she could think of something to say, Jake appeared, a scowl still on his face. "Merry Christmas, you two. Have you been enjoying your morning?"

"Yes, we've been chatting away," Thalia replied, smoothing her hands over the book she'd been reading when Lily came in.

"I see Lily has been schooling you on her favorite subject. She is quite the expert on both pride and prejudice."

Lily furrowed her brow, only then noticing his grandmother had been reading a copy of Jane Austen's *Pride and Prejudice*. She rolled her eyes at his attempt at sarcasm.

"It's too bad you weren't reading *Sense and Sensibility*, Thalia. Sometimes Jake could use a bit of both."

Thalia laughed as Jake's scowl deepened. "I think perhaps you both could use a little *Persuasion*. Anything to get you in a festive mood before tonight."

Jake's harsh demeanor lifted. "The two of you have decided to band together. How am I supposed to compete with that?"

"You're not, darling." Thalia smiled up at him, adoration evident in her gaze. "Just appreciate that we get on so well. I can't wait to introduce her to everyone tonight."

"What happens tonight?" Lily asked.

"My grandmother invites everyone she knows to dinner and gets to tell them how wonderful I am. It's the highlight of her year, isn't it?"

"I'm not as bad as all that usually, but this year you'll have to forgive me. My grandson is getting married and I'm thrilled." She folded her hands in her lap and turned to Lily. "We'll exchange our gifts before everyone else arrives. In fact, with so much to look forward to, I think I'll have a rest now. I want to be fresh for tonight."

"Would you like me to help you?" Lily asked, concerned since the nurse was absent.

"No need, dear." She accepted Jake's arm as she stood and then smiled at them both. "Besides, I think the two of you need some time to yourselves."

Lily forced a smile, knowing what she wanted was anything but time alone with Jake, especially with her mind so muddled.

"I'm going to check out a few properties on a neighboring island tomorrow and we'll fly home the next day. I'm sure you're in a hurry to get away." Jake wrapped his hands on the railing and looked out without seeing anything. His mind hadn't stopped working since last night, and still he was no closer to a solution. He'd hoped looking in on the families that kept an eye on his grandmother might shine a light on his own problems, but they'd only darkened his mood.

"There's no need to rush back on my account. Unless there is something you need to do, someone you need to see."

He turned around, pinning her to the chair with his gaze. "Is there something you want to ask me, Lily? Or would you rather be cool and flippant? I suppose it doesn't matter since you make up your own story anyway."

"What would you have me do? Live in the dark? You obviously don't trust me with the truth."

"You don't trust me at all, so I suppose that makes us even."

"Yes, we do seem to be equally miserable, don't we?" She pulled her bottom lip between her teeth in a gesture he'd come to learn meant she had more to say, so he waited until she spoke again.

"Your grandmother told me about your father."

He nodded and narrowed his eyes. "Is that why you were sitting with her, pumping her for information so you could be justified in thinking me beneath your notice? I told you he was a troll. Did you need more details than that?"

"Would you stop putting words in my mouth? I'm not some elitist using that as an excuse not to marry you. You don't love me and you'll never care to. It's as simple as that." Lily stood, smoothing her hands on her white slacks. "I was merely going to ask why you feel responsible for so many. I've only ever had to look after myself, and you had to teach me how to do that, so I don't understand why you hold yourself accountable for others."

Jake watched her as she stood perfectly still and poised, as if she hadn't just asked the hardest question he'd ever had to answer. "What exactly did my grandmother tell you?"

"Enough so that I know you only tell me what suits you. I do find it strange that you can rail at me for acting jealous about Mikayla and then turn around and instigate it by saying you're going out with her."

"I did—"

"Drive her to her parents' house? Really, Jake, your definition of the truth needs a little work. You said you would always be honest with me, but can you even count the number of times you've lied?"

He shook his head. "I've never lied to you. Some of your invented stories have been so ridiculous they didn't deserve a rebuttal. It's not my fault if you believe your own fiction."

"I suppose the blame is all mine. I've known better from the very beginning. I think your grandmother had the right idea. I'd like to rest before the party tonight."

She walked past him and he fought the urge to grab her, to communicate with her on the one level they always connected on. But he couldn't, not trusting himself to stop before it went too far.

"Jake?" He looked up at Lily as she stood, one hand on the glass door leading inside. "I need to know how to act at the party. Will we be pretending to be in love tonight?"

For the first time in over a decade he felt a pressure behind his eyes and a betraying tightness in his throat. Instead of speaking, he shook his head and turned around, wondering just how he could have allowed one small woman to bring him so low.

Lily watched the sun bounce on the surface of the sea, looking for answers she knew she'd never find. Jake Tolliver was an enigma, and trying to understand him or how she felt about him only led to a headache.

She turned back to the room, checking her reflection in the full-length mirror angled against one wall. The cream pleated chiffon of her dress swirled to mid-thigh, a black satin bow highlighting the empire waist. Even with her hair twisted to one side, she thought she looked too young. Youth could be an asset, but it seemed to make Jake's women dismiss her on sight. Really, what she needed was a tight red number, but spending money on clothes was out of the question right now. Besides, Hawaii was more casual than most places and she was here to meet his grandmother after all.

She didn't need to worry about Jake's women dismissing her. He seemed to have done that himself. It cut like a knife, but she knew it was for the best for them both. Now that she knew more about his past, she knew he'd never be able to give up the others, never be able to commit himself fully to one person. He'd never had a single person to trust, had never been shown how to rely on anyone but himself.

While she'd spent a lifetime trusting others to care for her and indulging herself. The last few months had turned that on its ear, but she was an intrinsically trusting person. So much so she sometimes forgot to protect herself from what she felt for Jake.

Not that it would matter now. Even he'd given up his relentless pursuit. Lily walked to the bed where she'd laid out the gifts she'd brought, her mind falling back to the thoughtful gifts Jake had bought her in the past. This was the first time she'd ever had anything to give him in return.

Laughter in the other room caught her attention. Mikayla's trill cackle wafted through the walls and Lily steeled herself against the night. She knew how to do this, mingle at parties and pretend to be having the time of her life. What she was unsure of as she gathered the gifts was how to keep Jake believing she was as indifferent to him as he thought while Mikayla wrapped herself around him.

Lord help her, she *was* jealous. And in love. A feeling as unknown and exhilarating as it was dangerous. She was about to act the part for the world, while maintaining her indifference to the man she loved. An actress with a shelf of awards would probably be just as nervous as she as she made her way to the great room.

Of course, Mikayla stood next to Jake, her hand on his arm as she posed in an exquisite emerald gown. To his credit, he excised himself from the situation and was by Lily's side with a glass of champagne by the time she'd set her gifts next to the others on the table.

"We should have a toast before the crowd arrives." The resignation in his voice rang oddly in her ears. She took the glass from him, her fingers tingling where they touched.

"It's not a crowd, Jakob. Just my closest friends." Thalia grinned from her chair.

"You have over a hundred close friends, and those are just the ones coming tonight." He pasted on an indulgent smile, but Lily could tell it was forced.

"Really, Jakob. You're going to scare Lilianna."

The corner of his mouth twitched. "Lily doesn't scare easily. She may look slight, but she can work a crowd of socialites better than both of us combined. Too bad it's Christmas, or you could have had her bleeding the wallets of everyone for your literacy project."

Lily pursed her lips together, unsure what to make of the backhanded compliment. "I don't make anyone's wallet bleed."

His gaze dripped over her from head to toe, making her squirm in her kitten heels. "You do make people think huge donations are their idea, so I'm sure they don't notice. At least the husbands don't."

Thalia laughed, cutting the tension. "A fool and his money are soon parted, right dear? Especially when the man has enough money to do some good. It's one of the finer points of fundraising."

Jake looked from his grandmother to Lily and smiled, a true one this time. "I'm never going to win between the two of you, am I? All right then, we'll drink to that. Lily, what was the toast your father did?"

Her throat thickened as the image of her father looking down from the staircase on their guests at last year's party flashed in her mind. She put the staggering wave of emotion aside and lifted her glass.

"May you never forget what is worth remembering, and never remember what is best forgotten." They all took a sip which gave Lily a chance to step out of her grief.

"Now for my favorite part," Thalia said. "The presents."

"I think that is everyone's favorite part of Christmas." Lily passed out her gifts as everyone took a seat on the sofas. When Thalia opened the package, her eyes welled up as she stared at the silver frame.

"How did you manage such a lovely portrait? Jakob hates to have his picture taken."

Lily grinned, watching as Jake stretched to see the picture she'd given his grandmother. "It's from a benefit ball last year. I don't think he knew it was being taken."

"I didn't." He leaned back in the seat next to her and lowered his voice. "I was too busy looking at you."

Her cheeks heated at the insinuation. Lily took the last of her gifts from the table and handed the oblong package to him.

"You got me something?" Jake said under his breath.

"It's about time, don't you think?" she whispered back.

He stared at her with a bewildered expression that shamed her to her core. After all he'd been through, having been so coldly treated by her in the past had to have been an icy slap in the face. She hadn't known, and she couldn't take it back, but she wanted to all the same.

He peeled back the silver paper with precision. Each second was torturous as she waited to see if she'd done the right thing. Jake lifted the stacked frames from the paper and set them side by side on his lap, never saying a word.

Finally, Lily couldn't take it anymore. "It's just a print, I didn't damage the original. I promise."

"What is it, Jakob?" Thalia asked, leaning forward. Mikayla followed suit.

Jake turned the frames to face the other women. "It's the floor plans and renderings of the house, the originals on one, and a remodel idea I had on the other."

"That house is huge." Mikayla exclaimed. If Lily hadn't been so worried by Jake's reaction, she might have smiled.

"It's gorgeous, Jakob." Thalia reached out for the frames so he set them in front of her. "Why are you changing it?"

He opened his mouth to respond, but shut it again and turned, his gaze piercing through Lily. "The house isn't set up for a family, so one day I played with moving the master suite upstairs. Where did you find the plans?"

"In your desk at the penthouse. Planning needed the River House designs and they weren't in the office and I knew you'd taken them home, so I had to go find them and came across these at the same time." She pressed her fingernails into her palms, trying not to panic. Even if he were truly angry at the intrusion, he wouldn't yell at her in front of his grandmother. Would he? "I thought you could hang these at the penthouse so you could think of the house while you are in town during the week."

"Do you like the changes?" There was a pensive gleam to his eyes, an anxiety in his tone she never would have imagined him capable of if she hadn't witnessed it.

Lily raised one shoulder. "I'm used to my bedroom the way it is, but you do have a point. It was fine for me because Emmaline slept upstairs when I was younger, but without a nanny it could be quite the hassle."

"Yes. You'd wind up staying upstairs with the baby and I'd be alone."

Lily opened her mouth in shock, taken aback as Jake covered her mouth with his own. The gentleness of his lips on hers was an equal surprise. She didn't mind a bit that he'd done it in front of Mikayla, but she worried about what his grandmother might think. The restraint in the kiss made her want to deepen it and relieve the hostility between them, but she didn't dare for more reasons than she could count.

Still reeling from the kiss, she barely noticed what the others gave or received. Thalia's gift of a bracelet linked with gold Plumeria blossoms touched her heart, and would always help her remember Hawaii. Jake gave her earrings that matched the diamond necklace.

Guests began to arrive before she got her head together. Thalia kept her close, introducing her to more people than she'd ever be able to remember. The Christmas gathering became a celebration of the engagement that wasn't real, and if she hadn't been so busy she might have rued the bittersweet event. As it was, the activity was just the cure for her emotional day. She was too busy trying to make conversation and remember how the families fit together to worry about how she felt about missing her parents, Jake's kiss or how life would change when she went home.

Her feet were aching by the time she felt Jake's hand on her arm, propelling her to the secluded lanai. Lily was thankful for the fresh air and the chance to sit in quiet for a moment. Jake's intent stare made her nervous, so she didn't want to indulge for too long.

"We should get back inside. People will wonder what happened to us." She watched him warily as he sat down beside her.

"No, they won't. We just announced our engagement, disappearing together is par for the course." The grin on his face aroused old fears and insecurities. She'd thought him too angry to continue pursuing her, but his actions tonight seemed more genuine than forced. Really, she'd never know where she stood with him until they were miles apart.

"The engagement is to make Thalia happy, so we should go in and do that." Lily tried to get up, but he stopped her with a hand on her thigh.

"I'm having a hard time with it. I need another minute."

Maybe he didn't lie as smoothly as she thought. "We can tell her the truth after they all leave if it's bothering you. That way it will be in person."

He narrowed his eyes. "Not that. I don't like the way men look at you. I honestly thought a ring on your finger would help."

"You did?" Her voice rose in surprise.

"I know men aren't always the most scrupulous, but yes, I thought it would get rid of this feeling." He rolled his shoulders and stretched his long legs in front of him, as if he could release his discomfort like a tight muscle.

"What feeling is that?" Lily asked, truly confused now.

"Like I need to put myself between you and every other man in the room to keep you from leaving with one of them." His voice was gruff, as if he were disgusted with himself.

"It's probably your own guilt you're feeling." Lily picked at the pleats of her dress.

"I don't have anything to feel guilty for."

"Your conscience seems to think otherwise." She smiled, hoping she didn't sound chastising. She understood now why he'd never be able to put all his faith in one person, but that didn't mean she approved. "I don't want to fight about this today. Christmas is a holiday and I think we should take a break from bickering as well."

"Agreed." Jake smoothed his hand along her temple and around the back of her head.

Her instinct was to pull away, but her side-swept hair was only held in place by two combs. She'd have to walk back through the house disheveled if he undid it, and since that was probably what he wanted she stayed still.

"I'm going to be very rude, and you're going to have to get over it."

"Am I really?"

He cleared his throat. "How did you afford Christmas gifts?"

She blinked at his bluntness and squared her shoulders. "I have a job. I didn't steal them if that's what you're thinking."

He loomed over her in the moonlight, his shadow covering her completely. "Of course you didn't. But you haven't paid your tuition completely and they're holding your diploma until you do. I paid you exactly enough to cover it. I expected you to use the credit card I gave you for everything else."

"You have no right to be looking into my account with the university." She tried to bat away the hand that held her, but he caught her attempt with his free one.

"You earned that degree and I'm not going to let something as trivial as money stand in the way of it."

"I have it taken care of."

"How?" His direct gaze showed her neither of them was moving until he got his answer.

"I'm going to sell some of my jewelry to pay it off. I don't need all of it, so downsizing is in order anyway. I should get enough to pay tuition and get an apartment."

He shook his head. "Will you at least sell it to me?"

"So you can give it back to me? No."

"You would put off getting a diploma it took you years

to earn just so you could buy Christmas gifts for me and my grandmother." His fingers splayed over the back of her neck, lulling her into a trance. "Your entire body responds at the smallest touch from me. And yet you swear you don't like me at all."

She swallowed hard, remembering how it tore her up to know she'd hurt him. She didn't want to do it again. "It's not that. There are moments where I see why you think we'd work out so well together, but I know better. I can't tolerate the way you live your life."

"Which part? Working, traveling—"

"The other women, Jake. You know that. There's no point teasing me about it."

"So we do have something to negotiate?"

She shot him a cold look. "This isn't a business deal. I won't budge on what I need. I understand why you can't either. It's an impasse."

"I don't know what you think you understand, but I know what I want and there is nothing I won't do to get it."

He brought her to him in a kiss so fiery and passionate she didn't even want to pull away. Still, it had that underlying gentleness that was her complete undoing. Her hands moved of their own volition, first to his cheeks, then to the collar of his shirt.

"Oh no, I didn't think I'd interrupt you." Mikayla's barefaced lie had Lily clinging to the fabric of Jake's shirt. "Joe Akana wants to settle on the time he's flying you to Niihau tomorrow. Are you really going to buy land there?"

To his credit, Jake didn't look up at the other woman. "Tell Joe I'll be inside in a minute."

Lily stared up at Jake, relaxing her hands as she heard Mikayla's retreating footsteps. "I'm trying not to hate her."

"Next time we come it will be easier."

"Jake, there won't be—"

He silenced her with a finger to her lips. "I don't want to get into it here. When we're back home we'll discuss everything."

Lily let her shoulders droop in defeat as he returned to the house. She loved him completely. It was going to be the greatest struggle of her life not to compromise and let him have things his way.

Chapter Eleven

A balmy breeze wafted up the hill, carrying with it the rustle of leaves and the eternal song of the ocean waves. The heady scent of plumeria perfumed the entire veranda. Lily leaned back on the chaise enjoying the heat of the day.

Soon enough she'd be back home, wondering if the day would bring rain, snow or a mixture of both. Until recently she'd never considered living anywhere else, but somewhere warm would be a plus. Maybe it would distract her from the lost feeling she had whenever Jake was gone. Even now, relaxing in paradise, she wished she'd have found some reason to go with him.

With a sigh, Lily began to wonder if when it came down to it she'd actually be able to move on. She knew she'd never marry him, but she couldn't actually see herself leaving him either. She tried to read the book she'd carried outside after lunch, but tiny yellow birds hopping from one feathered fern to the next were far more interesting.

A glass shattered inside the house, catching her attention. Lily rose and walked inside. Thalia sat in a cane chair, clutching her chest, her face pale. Lily rushed to her, careful of the shards beneath her feet. Mikayla raced into the room with a glass of water in one hand and two bottles of pills in the other as Lily reached the older woman.

Confused by the situation, Lily could only watch as Thalia struggled to gulp down one pill and then hold another beneath her tongue. She held Thalia's hand, her gaze bouncing between the two women. Neither of them looked at her, they were both mesmerized by the television. Lily tried to see what caught their attention on the midday news, but the weather couldn't have caused this kind of reaction.

"Do we need to call someone?" Lily asked, wondering what kind of attack Thalia was having.

"Don Kalama," Thalia got out on a whisper. "He'll know who to call. Maybe he'll even go looking."

Lily knit her brows, more baffled than ever. "Who is—"

"Sshh!" Thalia held up her hand as the news anchor appeared on the screen again.

The words Lily heard sent an icy chill down her spine. Helicopter crash. Into the ocean. Four missing. Pilot Joe Akana radioed a hydraulic problem.

Her body tensed and froze at the familiar name. The man she'd seen talking with Jake last night. About flight arrangements. She forced herself to breathe, wanting nothing more than to run into the ocean herself.

"If you'll stay with her, I'll call Don."

Lily blinked to awareness, nodding at Mikayla. It

wasn't as if she could go anywhere, the older woman's grip on her hand had tightened like a vice. Her pursed lips had gone white, making Lily doubly nervous.

"We need to stay calm, Thalia. Until we know something, we can't think the worst." Lily was glad for the numbness taking over her body, it almost made her voice steady. "He's a very strong swimmer. I once watched him swim laps for almost an hour."

Thalia's face softened. "I'm glad he found you, Lily. He so deserved to be happy." She tried to say more, but emotions overran her and she began to cry. It was all Lily could manage not to join her.

"Don's going to make some calls and get back to us." Mikayla came into the room and placed a hand on Thalia's shoulder. "You need to lie down. I called Dr. Ferber and he'll be by within the hour."

Thalia merely nodded, allowing the nurse to help her out of the room. Lily was thankful for the broken glass. It gave her something to do with her body while her mind reeled. Jake was a strong swimmer, her covert appreciation of him had taught her that. But swimming out from a helicopter crash was entirely different than laps in the pool at the house.

She sank onto the couch after cleaning up, pulling her knees to her chest as she stared at the television. The newscast had ended, a daytime game show was trying to spread happiness in a house where there was none.

She should have gone with him. If he could make a case for her tagging along to sites in the snow, she could have talked him into it. But she'd wanted to avoid him, wanted to keep him thinking she wasn't consumed with love for him, wanted to get away from the powerful pull that had her dreaming about marrying a man with an inscrutable view of marriage vows.

Bitter tears tracked down her cheeks as she gave in to the emotions swirling around her. She'd lost him too. Losing her mother before she got a chance to know her always had Lily feeling alone. Her father's death was still a fresh wound, one Jake had done so much to help heal. Losing him as well was too much to bear. With her mother she'd been too young to realize what was happening, her father's illness had given them time to say goodbye, but this?

How could she ever forgive herself for not letting him know how she felt? Anger blazed within at her own stubbornness. With the life Jake had lived, how could she have added to the list of people who withheld their affection and approval from him? It made her as bad as his parents and more ashamed of herself then she'd ever been.

She covered her face with her hands, the engagement ring rubbing against her cheek. She looked down at the ring, glad she'd done at least that much for him.

Lily sat frozen on the couch, numb as the local channel ran through their daytime schedule with little news of the accident. She regained her composure as people came to the house. The doctor even brought her a bottle of pills to help her sleep, but she didn't want to dream so she didn't dare try them.

Each time she heard a slamming car door from outside she cringed they might finally bring the news she feared. By nightfall they'd gotten word three of the passengers had been rescued and were recovering at the hospital. Since they hadn't been informed Jake was among them, Lily was grateful his grandmother had been given a sedative. She knew she'd have to, but she wasn't sure how she'd break the news to Thalia. It was one thing to have to think of life without him, quite another to give voice to such drive and vitality being snuffed out for no reason at all.

"Lily, I'm going to go to bed. Is there anything you need before I turn in?" Mikayla's sympathetic smile had little effect.

Lily shook her head. "Will Thalia be all right?"

"For the night. The doctor will be back in the morning. You will stay, won't you?"

"Of course." It was the least she could do for a man who'd done so much for her.

She sat for a few more minutes, her mind starting to work through a list of all the people she'd need to call tomorrow with the news. She didn't want to go there yet, didn't want to make it true when it still felt unreal. She wandered outside and looked up at the night sky. The moon glowed big and ripe, stars twinkling in a sky so soft it looked like velvet.

Geckos chirped and the sound of the surf was louder now that night had taken over for the busy day. Headlights turned up the drive and her stomach tensed again. She realized how much she'd appreciated Mikayla's detached interference throughout the day. Now it was solely up to her to get whatever details were to be provided and relay them to Thalia in the morning.

The car slowed and Lily's heart skipped a beat as she caught sight of the passenger. Her feet froze in disbelief for a moment, but she decided if she had fallen asleep and started to dream she was going to live this one out fully.

She broke out into a run as the car door opened, her mind seeing nothing but Jake as he climbed out and stared at her. He looked just as he had this morning at breakfast, as if a day of panic hadn't touched him at all.

She launched herself into his arms when she was close enough, squeezing him until she knew he wasn't in her imagination. His scent of sun and soap filled her lungs, giving her the first taste of calm she'd had in hours. In that moment of reprieve, her vow not to let herself become undone by him shattered. She was his to do with what he would, for all the moments time allowed them.

"Thanks, Don." Jake's voice vibrated through her, but she couldn't let go. Not yet. The car drove away and yet they stayed rooted on the grassy drive.

"I was so afraid," she whispered against his chest. "When I saw the car I thought they'd found you and I'd have to tell her."

His posture straightened, tension palpable within him. "Thalia is a strong woman, and Mikayla can take very good care of her."

Lily eased her grip just enough to be able to look up at him. "What happened to you?"

"Joe dropped me off on Niihau. He got into some trouble on the way back, but Don says they'll all be fine."

"You weren't on the helicopter when it crashed?"

He shook his head. "I didn't know there'd been a crash until Don landed on the island. I thought it was best to come straight home rather than phoning first. Is Thalia still awake?"

"She should be out until morning. Mikayla had a doctor come and check her and they gave her a sedative."

He nodded. "Okay. You should get some rest."

"I can't." She held him tighter, hating the trembling need in her voice. "I thought you were gone and I was truly alone this time."

"None of that now. I'm here." He took her face in his hands, wiping away tears she hadn't known she'd shed with his thumbs. "You'd be fine on your own. Maybe better even. You'd get the house."

"I don't want the house." She choked on a sob and buried her face in his chest again to try and hide.

Jake gathered her close, resting his head on her hair while she calmed down again. "If I'd known what was going on, I would have gotten word to you. This holiday was supposed to be peaceful and I've managed to throw both you and my grandmother into a panic."

"It's not your fault. Besides, we'll be fine now." She

took a deep breath and wiped her face.

He hesitated, measuring her for a moment. "Have you eaten anything today?"

She couldn't help the smile that came to her face. "I'm not going to faint, I promise. But you must be hungry, all day on that island."

"It's not deserted, just not open to the public. Hawaiian hospitality is wonderful, especially when they need your money. They want to have a few helicopters of their own, and the privacy would be unparalleled."

Panic seized her anew. "I don't want you in a helicopter for a while, okay?"

"I took one back." He grinned down at her. "You best be careful, Angel. I'm tempted to think there's a reason why you're so shaken."

Denying it now would be impossible. She reached down and slid his hand in hers. "Show me your bungalow."

"I don't think that's a good idea. I want us to talk once we get home. We'll sort it all out then, not here."

"You don't want to be with me?" Her chest tightened as she said the words of her greatest fear. Maybe the reason he knew he'd always need other women was because she'd never measure up to the ones he'd already known.

The heart-rending tenderness of his gaze eased her worries. "It's not that, Angel."

She took a few steps toward the path to the bungalow

and turned, still holding on to his hand. "Then show me the bungalow."

His body hummed with anticipation. Usually he was so in tune with her he could use her apprehension to rein himself in, but now he felt only eagerness. Whether his, hers or both of theirs, he didn't know, but he'd denied himself for so long her fervent willingness stretched his nerves until they were taut as bow strings.

He needed her and had for so long the ache had become a part of his existence. The thought that they might finally sate the urge filled his mind with the taste of her skin, the feel of her body beneath his. He took the lead as they walked to the bungalow not because he was entirely sure this was the right move to make, but because if he didn't move faster they might never make it up the stairs.

"It's like a tree house," Lily said as they rounded the bend in the path.

"It's on stilts, not in the trees. It makes for more privacy and a better view. Off the veranda you can lean over and pick bananas, avocados or papayas. It's like you're suspended above the world."

The urge to take the stairs two at a time was overwhelming, but he slowed his pace, letting Lily pause to look out at the jungle canopy as the stairs turned. Her profile in the moonlight taunted him. He wanted her with a desperation he'd never known, but he wanted her willing, not because her emotions were on overload after today's scare. Still, it had to mean something that she'd been upset, that she'd wanted to come with him at all.

He opened the door at the top of the stairs and turned on the light. He wondered about candles, about setting a scene for her, but decided to let her decide what she wanted.

She stood in the doorway, her shoulders relaxing as she smiled. "It's perfect. Open and romantic, but not overdone. You should do more original design work."

"It's more interesting to fix other people's mistakes or to bring back something that was too long neglected. Besides, there are too many possibilities in designing something new, unless you know exactly what you want." He took her hand and led her into the room. "Do you know what you want, Angel?"

She nodded, then turned and flipped off the light. "The moon is enough, and I don't want Mikayla to see the light is on and investigate."

"She's not—" Her soft finger against his lips stopped his explanation.

"In love with you? Yeah, I figured that out today, among other things." Her hands were trembling as she took his. "I'm in love with you and I have been for a while. You were right about me being jealous. I can hardly breathe when I think of you with someone else. But that doesn't matter now. All day I wished that I'd told you, that you'd known. I didn't want to lose you while you thought I was indifferent to you."

He pulled her closer. "You've never been indifferent.

There's a thin line between love and hate, we just need to keep you on this side."

"I never hated you, I swear. I couldn't handle my reaction to you so I lashed out. But I don't want to do that anymore. I want to be honest about how I feel."

"I love you too, Angel." His gut clenched as he squeezed her hands, knowing she told the truth. Finally, she loved him, which was what he'd wanted for so long.

Lily blinked, surprise lighting her eyes. "You don't have to—"

"I fell in love with you the first time I saw you. I sought you out to prove myself wrong, really. From the moment I touched you I knew that it was real, that no one else would ever do."

The admission made him feel raw and exposed. He didn't want to talk anymore, didn't want to risk the moment getting away from him. He raised his hands to her face, tilting it so that he could slide his mouth against hers. Her lips opened for him, her tongue circling his while her hands crept up his body to undo the buttons of his shirt.

He broke the kiss and fanned his thumbs along her cheeks. "What do you want, Angel?"

"I want you to make love to me. I want to fall asleep knowing that you're with me."

"We can just sleep if—"

"No. Please, don't reject me again." Her voice began to tremble. "If pity is all you have to give, I will take it."

His heart ached for her, for what they'd done to each other, for each other. "I've never pitied you, Lily. But I don't want to be something you regret."

She looked up at him, her eyes glistening. "I regret that we haven't been together already."

He had to trust her, here and now. He took her hand and led her across the room to bed. He lowered his head and kissed her again, smiling when her hands went back to the buttons on his shirt.

He covered her hands with his own. "Anticipation is one of the best parts of sex."

"I don't believe you." She grinned and a shiver of delight raced through him. "I think I want you to work at proving yourself wrong. We've had too much anticipation."

"There can never be enough. Don't you want me more now than you did before we came upstairs?" He undid the buttons of the white eyelet blouse she wore with deliberate slowness.

"Yes, but—"

"And now?" He pushed the shirt off her shoulders and then ran his fingers beneath the straps of her satin bra. He undid the front clasp, opening her up like a present.

She shook her head, her eyes gleaming with a brazenness he'd never seen. Her fingers made quick work of his buttons and pushed his shirt away. She took a step closer so that the hardened tips of her nipples brushed against his chest. She closed her eyes, tilted her head to one side and began to sway, each subtle movement grazing against him.

"Now I want you more." Her lips quirked in a seductive grin. She opened her eyes and wrapped her arms around his neck. "If you lose the pants, I'll let you have your way with me." She leaned closer until he could feel her breath against his ear. "If you take much longer I might even beg."

He groaned and dragged her down onto the bed. She kicked off her sandals along the way, making it easy for him to remove her white Capri pants. She wiggled away from him and got up on her knees.

"Do you need some help?" She reached for his jeans and he tried to let her undo the buttons, clenching his jaw as her fingers brushed against him. Finally it was too much and he stood up to finish the job himself. Mischief gleamed in her gaze as she watched his every move.

"You like what you see?"

She shrugged, causing her pert breasts to bounce in invitation. "You're the first man I've gotten to see naked. I'm curious."

"Are you?" He rid himself of the rest of his clothes and then joined her on the bed. He was painfully aroused, but he knew she'd need to go slow. He lay down and propped himself up on one elbow, smiling as Lily faced him and did the same thing.

The intimacy and safety of being with Jake wrapped around Lily like a drug, lulling her to brazen euphoria. "I don't just read proper literary novels. There are things I've read about that have made me wonder."

"Like what?"

"Like if you can really taste someone's pulse thrumming in their neck." She dipped her head, kissing his neck until she could indeed feel his pulse beneath her tongue. When she looked up he wore an intoxicated smile that encouraged her to indulge. "And whether you'd feel the way I do when I touch your nipples." She inched down and flicked her tongue against one flat disk, grinning as it peaked when she blew across it.

"Yours are better." He palmed one breast, rubbing his thumb across the sensitive tip.

"Why? Because bigger is better?"

He laughed, rolling them over so that he was on top, his muscular thigh sliding between her legs. "You're amazing."

"I want to feel amazing." Her body filled with such a charge of excitement, a frantic rush of desire to be with him completely flooded through her. He was here, and alive, and in this moment he was hers completely.

She indulged her every desire to touch him, to feel the corded and bunched power of his muscles beneath his warm skin. She wanted to learn his body, but thought flew from her mind as his hands began their own exploration.

Skilled expertise won out and she gave herself over to the heady flash of sensations he rained down on her body. She threaded her hands through his hair while his mouth worked her nipple until her legs began to twitch. His fingers plucked at the bud while he turned his attentions to her other breast. She twisted and bowed her body, trying to ease the ache that came from not receiving what she really craved.

He must have sensed her frustration because soon one hand was tugging down her panties. She wriggled her hips to help him, thankful when she could kick them off the side of the bed and be completely bare to him. His hand slipped between her thighs and she relaxed them open, enjoying the warmth spreading throughout her body.

His fingers played her body like a finely tuned instrument, showing her nuances of pleasure she'd never imagined. While he strummed the bud of her sex, his finger slid inside of her, filling her with the most exquisite sensation.

The feel of his skin beneath her hands wasn't enough, so she reached for him, bringing his face to hers for a kiss deeper than any she'd ever experienced. Another finger stretched her and she opened herself for it the way she did for his kiss. She moaned into his mouth as her hips began to rock in time with his ministrations. He moved within her, the pleasure reaching a crest that broke all around her, sending warm tingles throughout her body and filling her mind with pure bliss.

His hands roamed up her body, leaving quivering trails of desire in their wake. From beneath her lust-induced fog she tangled her legs with his, trying to pull him as close as possible.

"Please, Jake." Already her body was throbbing for more, throbbing for him. She'd never imagined it would be this way, that she could feel so safe and out of control at the same time. Running her hands down the smooth muscles of his back, she found the rise of his bottom and pulled him against her.

"Are you ready?" his voice rasped in her ear.

"Yes, please, yes," she whispered on a moan.

He moved over her, his body pressing hers into the soft mattress until she felt the weight of him solid above her. His erection pushed against her, rubbing along her swollen sex. She tilted her hips, watching his eyelids lower at the movement.

It gave her a rush that he wanted her too. She wanted him completely, needed to know he was fully hers if only for a moment. His dark gaze locked with hers as he shifted and began the slow slide into her.

Knowing he was filling her made her heart swell with triumph and love. Surely he could see how she felt now. He'd never again have to doubt her devotion. He pumped his hips against her, the friction building her pleasure once again.

"You're mine, Lily."

"Yes." She lifted one leg and wrapped it around his hips. Now every move he made pressed right there, pushing her toward climax.

"No one else will ever have you but me."

"Yes." It was the truth. Her heart belonged to him, now and always. His dark passion drove her deeper into pleasure until it seemed too much to bear. She thought she might not be able to take any more, but at that

213

moment all the tension in her body released. She gasped, clutching at the sheets as her vision narrowed, stars dancing behind her eyes.

She heard Jake cry out as his hips jerked against her. Lily wrapped her arms around his neck, holding on with all the strength she had left.

Terror gripped her throat as the dream swirled around her. Lily opened her eyes, praying for reality. Her heartbeat steadied as she stared at Jake's bare chest, the intoxicating scent of him filling her lungs. The nightmare was over, completely.

Birds twittered outside, the early morning light just beginning to wake them. She ran her hands across the smooth lines of his chest, knowing she needed to get back to the house, to share the good news with Thalia so the older woman wouldn't be shocked by seeing her grandson alive.

But she couldn't let him wake up alone, not after last night. She nuzzled into his neck, kissing the saltiness from his skin. She wished she had half his skill, maybe in time she'd learn how to wake him up so that he'd open his eyes wanting her.

"Careful, Angel." Jake's voice was rough with morning. "As much as I'd love to stay here all day, we do have to go to the house."

"A few more minutes, then I'll go. I'll tell her and then you can come in, that way she won't get a shock." She grinned up at him and then rested her head on his chest so she could hear his heart beating. Today it was the most reassuring sound in the world.

"You are more amazing than I thought you would be."

She giggled. "Glad I could exceed your expectations."

His hand swatted her butt beneath the sheet. "That too, but I meant who you are. I'm still sorry for how scared you both must have been yesterday, but I'm glad you were here for Thalia."

"Me too." Lily lifted her head, pulling her bottom lip between her teeth. "You know, if you're still free on New Year's Eve, we could stay here."

"Why Lily Harris, are you proposing to me?" His gaze clung to hers, studying her reaction.

"Only if you're planning on accepting."

"Where's my ring?" He grinned, running his fingers through her hair.

"Would you wear one?"

His brows knit together. "Of course. We can pick one out today. I'm glad you're willing to get married so soon. A few months ago I'd have thought you'd want to put on a show of a wedding, but now I know something here would suit you more."

"And you. Besides, we'll come back here often so we can relive the memory over and over. At some reception hall things can be torn down as quickly as they go up."

"That's very romantic of you, but you don't have to convince me. After last night, I don't want to wait too long. Thalia is sharp, she could do the math and might slap me on the back of the head."

Lily laughed at the image. "What for?"

"We didn't use anything last night, Lily. You could be pregnant right now."

His smile had her blood chilling in her veins. Lily sat up, taking the sheet with her. "I'm not pregnant."

"Maybe not, but you could be."

She couldn't let him get his hopes up for a baby, now or ever. "Jake, I'm not. I went to the health center at the university and I got a birth-control shot."

"When?"

"After the night in the kitchen. It seemed to be the responsible thing to do."

He nodded. "It makes sense, besides it will happen when the time is right."

Lily looked about the room for her clothes, not wanting to leave him, but not wanting to disappoint him either. She knew her limits and had stretched them as far as they would go. There was nothing she wouldn't do for him, but that was her choice. A child would change everything. If she were a mother she'd have to put the child's need for security above her own desire for love.

"What is it, Lily? There's something going on behind those brilliant eyes of yours."

It was only fair to tell him, so she turned and braced herself for the disappointment in his eyes. It would come, but she wouldn't bend to it.

"I love you, Jake. I truly do. But I won't have children

with you." She swallowed hard, her mouth having gone dry.

"Why is that?" His dark gaze narrowed, shrewdly examining her.

"I won't raise a child in the kind of life we'll lead. It's not right."

A muscle clenched along his jaw. "I don't understand."

"I talked with Thalia and she explained a lot of things for me, about your parents and why you are the way you are."

"You don't want to have children with me because of my father? My God, what did she tell you?"

"I understand how your parents failed you, how—"

"And you think I would fail my children?" Jake jumped from the bed, pacing about the room as he picked up his clothes and tossed Lily's toward her. "I'm good enough to warm your bed, but not to father your children. How long do you plan on staying married to me, Lily? I'm not interested in being your first husband."

"You don't understand." Lily stared down, wringing her hands in her lap. "Children need security. They need to know where their father sleeps at night."

"Excuse me?"

"I'm willing to accept what you offer. I won't promise to like it, but I will live with it. But I will not bring a child into a life like that. If I had a daughter and she made this choice, it would break my heart to know that was the lesson I taught her."

"Then why is it enough for you?" Jake spat the words at her as if she were making the wrong choice.

"Because I love you, and I understand why you need more than one person to love you to fill up what they never gave you."

"You don't think you're enough?" The venom in his voice hit her like a slap.

"I wish I were." Tears stung her eyes as she played with the ring he'd put on her finger.

"Wish again. You didn't get the first one right." The bed sank where Jake sat next to her. His fingers slid beneath her chin, lifting her face until she was forced to look him in the eyes. "Go ahead and ask me. I'll defend myself this once. But I won't spend our lives doing it. If you can't trust me then it's not going to work anyway."

"How can you expect me to trust you when you've made it clear all along you intend to take a mistress whenever you want?"

He shook his head. "I never said that. You accused me of it."

"You didn't deny it!"

"I'm denying it now. There will be no one else, for either of us."

It felt like her mind was caught in the spin cycle. She'd spent the last month struggling to come to terms with this, and he was saying it wasn't an issue. "What about Dee?"

"Dee is my friend. I've known her since high school and I financed her boutiques, but that's all."

"But the papers said—"

"And they will again. I can't control that. That's why it's important that you believe me now."

She knit her brow, wanting more than anything for this to be the truth. "Dee said—"

"I can't control that either. I don't know what she implied, but she did it in hopes of protecting me. She thinks you're after my bank account."

Lily sat up straighter. "I don't want your money."

"I know. But Dee can't understand what your other motivation could be." His sardonic grin caught her off guard.

"You really haven't slept with her?"

He shook his head. "I'm not saying I've always lived like a monk, but since I met you there's been no one else."

That couldn't be. She'd seen pictures, read articles, had witnessed firsthand the way he was with other women. She tilted her head, trying to put it all together. Was she only believing him because she wanted it to be true? Mikayla's detached behavior yesterday and Thalia's opinion came together to show Lily she'd been wrong about that relationship, maybe she'd read too much into the others as well.

She stared up at him. "Why would you let me believe that?"

He shrugged. "You wanted to. We had so many battles

to fight, I didn't think starting there would be productive."

"You had Dee to the house."

He rolled his eyes. "You invited her."

"I thought—" She rubbed her face with her hands. "I don't know what I thought."

"You were jealous, and while we're confessing things, I baited you into it. Jealousy was the only encouragement you gave me, and so I took it."

"Why not just tell me the truth?" She watched as his face clouded with apprehension.

"Would you have believed me? Even now, after all we've shared you're still struggling."

"You don't know that."

"Yes, I do. Without trust you can't believe anything. My parents had their issues, but trust was the big one. He always thought there were other men. It didn't matter what she said or what she did. He didn't trust her and so he couldn't believe her. If you don't trust me there's nowhere for us to go."

"And you trust me? You were just as jealous about Ian."

"I trust that you know yourself, or I did until you told me why we're not having children."

"I thought it was the only way, the only solution I could live with."

"You couldn't have lived like that."

She closed her eyes and smiled, her nerves finally calming. When she opened her eyes and looked up at him, everything fell into place. "Thank goodness I'll never have to find out."

"So you'll trust me?" The morning light glimmered over his handsome face like beams of pure happiness.

"At home. I've seen you get creative with the truth in business meetings."

He wrapped his arms around her and pulled her close. "Then perhaps I should fire you in hopes you forget that part."

"I don't have a job for much longer anyway. Your PA is coming back from maternity leave. Besides, I don't want to be too busy to enjoy living in the city."

He tilted his brow, looking at her with uncertainty. "You don't want to stay at the house?"

"The penthouse is more convenient for us both. It's close to your office and the university. We can go to the house on weekends. Anyway, it would be too much of a hassle to live there with such extensive remodeling going on."

"Do we have a reason to remodel?"

She nodded. "Not right away, but when the time is right."

He kissed her softly. "Thank you, Lily. You'll never regret it, I promise."

"I know. I once made a deal with the devil and wound up in heaven instead."

About the Author

Jenna Bayley-Burke is a domestic engineer, freelance writer, award-winning recipe developer, romance novelist, cookbook author and logic-puzzle fanatic. Blame it on television, a high-sugar diet or ADD; she finds life too interesting to commit to one thing—except her high-school sweetheart, two blueberry-eyed boys and a perfect baby girl. Her stories, both naughty and nice, are available everywhere. To learn more about Jenna Bayley-Burke, please visit www.jennabayleyburke.com.

9 781609 280017